I0524236

CYNTHIA MELTON

Shayna

The Fate of the Faes, Book 1

By Cynthia Melton

Published by Take Me Away Books, an imprint of Winged Publications

ISBN-13: 978-1-0880-9748-9

DEDICATION

To those readers who like something a bit different

Character List:

Faeries

Shayna
Deema
Queen Linette
Earin
Alvar

Humans

Pierce Cochran
Clark Payson
Luke Marshal
Chief-of-Police Rosen

Other races

Kasdeya – demon
Radella – vampire
Seamus – leprechaun
Paddy – leprechaun
Gorna – dragon
Agatha – witch
Abaddon – Leader of the dark

1

Shayna

"You have to join the human world, Shayna. You're our best warrior." Queen Linette pounded her staff against the throne room's marble floor, sending sparks into the air. "Our very existence depends on their survival. Principalities are at work here that will destroy their world and ours. Already the human population has declined with an alarming rate, and those left are riddled with lust, violence, and immorality. Darkness is growing."

Shayna clasped her hands in front of her and gave a quick bow of her head. Deema. She had to be the one behind this.

"No, it's Radella, She has escaped her chains and is recruiting the dark fae and any other beast who will join her." Queen Linette said with a smile, reading Shayna's mind. "You must somehow convince Deema to join our side and re-enslave Radella. They're both already in the human world causing strife. Deema is the dark side's strongest warrior. Together, we can defeat the hold Kasdeya has on Radella and perhaps convince Deema to rejoin the Light."

"I won't be able to battle Deema into submission without making my true character known to the humans. The leprechauns will love alerting humans to my presence."

Queen Linette shook her head. "Doing so would also alert the human world to them." She leaned forward on her staff. "Find a human you can trust. Alert him or her to the danger of Kasdeya by any means. If the demons get control—well, I don't need to describe the chaos and obliteration of complete races."

"It's a lot of pressure on me, Queen. I'm strong but not battle proven. Am I to do it alone?" Shayna kept her eyes downcast but her posture rigid.

"You may engage any of the others who are willing to help you battle. The sprites are always happy to fight, but it is not time for our people to enter the fight as a group. A show of force will push Deema further away, lessening our chances of drawing her back to the Light."

Shayna gave a crooked smile. The sprites were mischievous for sure. At one time, they were responsible for most of the turmoil in the human world. Now that the demons had decided they wanted the humans for their slaves, the havoc the sprites caused dimmed in comparison to the evil spreading across the human world. "I'll leave now." She inclined her head and stepped back.

"You know what to do if you need help." The queen held out her hand.

Shayna grasped it. "I do."

"Do not bring a human into our world, Shayna. No matter what. You know the penalty."

"I know."

"Be careful, my sweet child."

"May I ask why me? We have other warriors." This time Shayna let her gaze meet that of her queen's.

"Because I know your heart is pure and cannot be corrupted by the darkness of Radella and Kasdeya as Deema's was. Our darker kin are so easily influenced."

True. The dark faeries were easily tempted by the riches the demons could give them. Shayna preferred the simple life of the fae of Light. Now, she had to enter the world of humans, a world full of corruption and immortality, in order to save a people who might not want to be saved.

"May the God of Light go with you," fae after fae said as Shayna made her way to her hut on the side of a cliff. Willow trees drooped overhead forming a cathedral. Filtered sunlight speckled the dirt path at her feet. Flowers in every hue of the rainbow broke up the expanse of green on each side of the path, filling the air with their fragrance. Fireflies flittered around her head. Such beauty.

Shayna sighed. Easy enough for the others to wish her well. None of them were leaving the beautiful glen they called home.

Passing under the curtain of a waterfall, Shayna entered her hut and donned her armor, buckling her sword to the blue belt around her waist, then adding a long, finely-woven rope of silver made of three braided strands, the strongest and finest the faeries had ever made. Fae rarely fought with weapons, preferring magic over the cruder form of battle, but Radella's people liked the physical fight and often prepared against magic.

Ready to battle, Shayna whistled, then leaped out her window onto the back of her winged horse, Crystal. "To the sprites."

Rather than the tall cliffs and waterfalls of the white fae, the sprites lived among large red wood trees in the flatlands. Shayna dismounted and pushed open the smooth wooden door and entered the head sprite's chambers.

When she stood and voiced her need before the tiny creature with sparkling blue skin, the sprite, Lita, shook her head. "Not now. We are not convinced the danger exists. Your queen is paranoid. When and if the need arises, you call on us with proof of this planet's demise, and we will come. You know the word."

She did. *Healp* would bring all creatures of the Light to her aid. Shayna bowed and backed out. A waste of time. She would enter the human world and hope she didn't perish alone in a strange world.

Shayna rode Crystal to the glimmering portal. One step and she could enter any world she wanted. All she had to do was say the word. She sent Crystal home, stepped through, and said, "New York."

Pierce

Detective Pierce Cochran thundered down the alley after the gang member with the canary-yellow purse. As the boy was climbing over a chain-link fence, Pierce grabbed him by the leg and pulled him down. "Joey, you know better." He whirled him around and cuffed him. "Come with me to return the purse before we head to the station."

"I ain't going nowhere with you, pig."

"You kiss your mother with that mouth?" Pierce hated street duty, but he'd been knocked down a couple of pegs after getting too rough with a punk who punched him. He shoved Joey ahead of him and marched him down 4th Avenue to where the victim waited.

The woman, dressed in a navy business suit and red heels, seized her purse, cast Joey a disgusted look, and rushed away. Ah, New York. Where people didn't take crap from anyone. A good thing, considering the alarming rate that crime was growing.

The moment he walked into the station and handed Joey over to be booked, the chief called Pierce into his office. "I'm putting you back to detective effective immediately. There's a body lying at a bar. Here's the address." He handed Pierce a slip of paper.

"Okay?" He raised his eyebrows.

"The patrolling officers said they've never seen anything like it. Officer Charges sounded shook up. Go see what in Hades is going on." Chief Rosen's chair creaked under his weight.

Charges was nothing but a rookie and easily

shook up. With a single nod, Pierce left and signed out one of the undercover squad cars. Thirty minutes later—no one went anywhere fast in New York traffic—he arrived to see an alley marked off with yellow crime-scene tape and three uniformed officers huddled in a tight group.

Frowning, he approached them. "What's up?"

"Dude, go take a look. It's like something out of a nightmare." The officer swallowed hard.

Pierce shot Charges a puzzled look and ducked under the tape. A young man, good-looking at one time, before his body had been drained of blood, lay next to a dumpster. No signs of a struggle. Nothing out of the ordinary except the unfastened zipper and lowered pants hinted at taking a leak or something hot and heavy with someone else. No blood, yet the man was as pale as the concrete beneath him and clearly dead.

Without touching the body, Pierce ran his gaze over the victim. Expensive suit, clearly a two-hundred-dollar haircut. He glanced at the back door of a strip club. As he started to stand, two puncture marks in the man's neck came into view. This was the third murder in a week made out to look like the attack of a fabled vampire. Since vampires didn't exist, it was obvious the department had a special kind of sick serial killer on their hands.

He returned to the other officers. "Have you spoken to those inside?"

"Yeah," Charges glanced at a notepad in his hand. "Didn't get much information, but the strip club manager..." he flipped through a notebook, "Rad Cooper, a real looker, too, said the man had been here and left around two a.m. Alone."

Pierce glanced up as a woman with waist-length raven hair and pale blue eyes stepped from the front entrance. The black leather pants and matching spaghetti-strap shirt accentuated her killer body and porcelain skin. Her cold gaze raked over Pierce before a sultry smile graced her lips. "That her?" He asked.

"Yep."

Pierce headed toward the woman as she opened the door to a black Jaguar. "Ma'am? I'd like to ask you a couple of questions."

Her cold gaze caused him to take a step back. What the hell? Pierce never let anyone intimidate him, much less a woman, yet his skin prickled at the ice in her gaze.

"I already told the others everything I know, which isn't much." Her husky voice furthered the chill running through his veins, but despite the frigid air around him, his body warmed, betraying him as a man's often did in the presence of a beautiful woman.

He cleared his throat. "I'd like to hear it for myself."

She sighed. "The man came in, had a few drinks, paid for a couple of lap dances, then left. Alone."

"Time?"

"Two a.m."

"You always note the time each customer leaves?"

"When it's a handsome one, yes." She slid into the driver's seat. "May I go?"

He nodded and handed her a business card. "Please call me if you remember anything that might help."

"Maybe I'll call you for a drink?"

Not on your life, lady. He forced a smile and watched her drive away, the warmth returning to the evening with her exit.

A flash of light emanated from the alley along with a sharp sound of thunder. Pierce broke into a sprint, skidding to a halt at the sight of a blond woman in black leggings and a shiny blue jacket standing over the body. "Hey, you can't be back here. This is a crime scene."

She whirled to face him, stopping him in his tracks at her beauty. Her eyes matched the blue of her jacket. Had to be contacts. No one had eyes that color. Rather than the disdain on the face of the club manager, this woman's face held a shadow of sadness.

"Who are you?" he asked.

"Shayna." Her soft voice sent his blood racing.

What was with the women he met today? Cold, warm, friendly, sad. He shook his head. "Shayna what?"

She blinked a few times, then said, "Sky."

"Shayna Sky." He'd bet his favorite pair of sneakers that wasn't her real name.

"Where do you come from?"

"The Glen."

Glen, New York, tiny town, beautiful scenery. "What brings you to New York City?"

"I'm looking for two people. Radella and Deema." She took a deep breath as if collecting herself and tried to pass him, sending one last mournful glance at the body. "I must be going."

He gripped her arm to stop her. "Do you know who killed this man?"

"Most likely Radella, considering the bite marks."

He raised his eyebrows. "Bite marks? Why?"

She shrugged. "That's what vampires do. She is dangerous, Mr...."

"Cochran. Detective Pierce Cochran." Despite his reluctance to give out information, he found himself answering her questions. Her eyes lured him like a fish. "I need you to come to the station with me." Loonier than a fruit bat. Why were the beautiful ones often short a bolt or two? He led her to his car and deposited her in the backseat, leaving the uniforms to wait for the ME. At the station, he took her to a small holding cell, handed her a business card and told her to sit, then closed the door behind him.

"Pretty lady," the chief said. "Who is she?"

"No idea, but I found her standing over the body. She said a vampire killed the guy." Pierce smirked. "She doesn't appear to be high or drunk, but something is definitely off about her."

Her head turned at his comment, and she stared at him through the small window in the door. Freaky. Almost as if she could hear him. Impossible through the heavy door. Her gaze flicked to the chief.

"Let her go."

"Sir?" Pierce stared into the chief's impassive face. The man looked hypnotized.

"She is an innocent." He pivoted and headed back to his office.

Pierce whipped around to face Shayna who now stood a breath away from the window. "Who are you?"

"Someone here to save you and your people."

Radella

Oh, he had smelled delicious. It had been all Radella could do not to drag him into her car, force him into sex, then drain him of blood as she used him to scratch the itch that had become her constant companion since being forced to join the side of the immortals three-hundred years ago. The fact she hadn't been able to influence him with her mind only made the detective more appealing. Not all men had darkness in their hearts. Some weren't enticed by the aura she sent out around her, but those men, thankfully for her, were becoming more and more rare. Although, feeding on one of the purer in heart quenched her hunger for a longer period of time.

She parked in a covered lot on Fifth Avenue and made her way to the penthouse where Kasdeya waited. It wouldn't do to be late, and Radella had only five minutes to spare.

The red-haired demon glanced at the clock on the wall as Radella entered the apartment. "Where is Deema?"

"Here." The dark fairy rushed into the room. Her fierce beauty almost dimmed the fire of Kasdeya and made Radella look washed out in comparison.

She shrugged. Perhaps years of avoiding more than a minimal amount of sunlight and drinking blood had paled her too much. The world's vampires had evolved to where early morning or early evening light didn't harm them, but Radella found old habits hard to break.

"Good." Kasdeya motioned for them to sit. "It seems we have a visitor from Linette's glen in our fine city."

Deema smiled. "Please tell me it's that goody, Shayna."

"It is." Kasdeya sat and crossed her long legs. "Those who carry the light are still strong. Do not underestimate the power Shayna brings with her. Most of the other world are still on their side, or neutral. They'll come if she calls. Her demise needs to be swift. I want the two of you to make sure that happens using whatever means necessary."

Radella was no fool. If Shayna was allowed to don her armor, the battle could rage for days.

Kasdeya narrowed her eyes. "Then, don't allow her to be battle-ready. Have you lost your nerve?"

"Of course not. My people fear no one."

A cold smile graced the demon's face. "Then why are you still sitting here?"

She glanced at Deema who shrugged. The two of them exited the penthouse, not speaking. For centuries the vampires detested the faeries and now Radella found herself partners with one. Radella sneered and headed for her car.

"Are you riding with me or alone?" She asked.

"Alone." Deema snapped her fingers and disappeared in an array of onyx-colored sparks.

Show off. Radella headed to her apartment where Deema was already waiting outside the door.

The fairy rolled her eyes. "So sad how the vampires lost their wings. What caused that?" She raised her eyebrows.

As if she didn't know that one of Radella's kind had killed the high priest, thus causing them to lose their ability to fly. "Who wants to turn into a bat anyway. Watch your tongue. Since I murdered your leader, I now control the dark faeries, and that includes you." Radella shoved her aside and unlocked the door, ushering the other woman into a dark room. With the press of a button, lamps glowed, casting a red glimmer over the black leather furniture. "Have a seat. Want a drink?"

"Anything besides blood?"

"Water, coffee, wine."

"Wine." Deema fell back onto the sofa and plopped her booted feet onto the glass-top table. "So, what's the plan?"

Radella handed her a glass of merlot. "What are a fairy's weaknesses?"

"The Light don't really have any, unless you count love." She took a sip. "They won't risk danger to humans if they can help it, so fighting in a crowd is best, since we don't care if a few humans die. There are too many of them anyway."

"Liar."

Deema smiled. "Which part?"

"Not caring. You're still a fairy and linked to the fate of man."

She shrugged. "True, but I value power more than love. While I won't murder a human on purpose, like you seem to thrive on doing, I can't help collateral damage. I'm also not stupid enough to tell you what can kill us."

"You'd better change that way of thinking if we're going to win a battle with Shayna." Radella hated the Light and craved the power its followers had. "We need to plan. When did she arrive?"

"Just minutes after your last kill."

Radella punched a code into a keypad on the wall and typed 666666, the code for her people to meet. With enough dark warriors, they could overtake one simple fairy. Right?

2

Shayna

Reeling from the disbelief and disappointment flickering in Detective Cochran's blue eyes, Shayna resumed her seat on the concrete bench of the holding cell. She could get free easy enough, but the concern for his people glowing from the detective's heart showed he could be the very man to help her. Only a pure heart could resist Radella and Deema. Traces of his meeting Radella wafted through him, yet he'd resisted her charms. Shayna would wait.

A few minutes later, Detective Cochran and two other men in dress shirts and ties stared in at her. She kept her face impassive and tried to ignore the conversation as clear as if the men stood in the same room with her. She also knew their names. Detectives Payson and Marshal. Good men, but struggling with issues of good and evil. She'd focus her attention on Cochran for now.

She stood and approached the window. "I'd like to get out now as the chief ordered."

Surprise flickered in Cochran's eyes. "This woman's hearing is amazing. Be careful what you say."

Marshal shook his head. "Weird stuff's happening in this city, and look at her eyes. That shade of blue isn't normal."

"Please." Shayna said. While those who followed the Light had patience, hers started to run thin.

Cochran sighed and unlocked the door. "I'll drive you home. We can't have you leaving town until you're cleared of murder."

"That won't take long since I've killed no one." She brushed past them, leaving three men breathless. Humans had so little restraint around beauty. "I will need a place to stay."

Cochran made a sound deep in his throat. "I know of a clean, reasonably-priced hotel."

"Price is not an issue."

"O-kay." He glanced at the other men. "I'll take you to the Ritz."

Maintaining a polite smile, she waved a hand for him to lead the way. "I'm sure with these two detectives watching, you don't need to fear I'll run."

Bright spots of color appeared on his chiseled cheekbones. "I'm not worried."

He led her to a dark blue Corolla and opened the front passenger door. Once she was seated, he climbed in the other side, then turned to her. "All right, Ms....Sky, but something about your story doesn't ring true. I want to know right now who you are, and I want the truth."

"I am Shayna, second-in-command to Linette, of the glen of Light."

"So, a whack-a-doodle." His features hardened.

"I don't know what that is, but no. I'm a faery."

Frustration spread across his handsome features. "Stop playing games. Faeries don't exist anymore than vampires."

"Yes, they do, just like demons, leprechauns, and sprites, to name a few." She sighed. "Take me to the hotel, Detective Cochran, and I will prove to you that I am telling the truth." She hadn't wanted to show him her wings so soon, but time was of the essence.

"Fine." He turned the key in the ignition and sped from the parking lot with a squeal of tires.

Shayna sat quietly and read his thoughts, deriving much-needed information as to what things around her were called. She needed to know a car from a taxi and a store from an apartment if she wanted to blend in. As for money, it had been easy enough to turn the detective's business card into a credit card.

"Do you have identification?" Cochran asked her.

"Like what?"

"A driver's license? State-issued I.D.?"

"Do you have another business card?"

He nodded and pulled one from his pocket.

She palmed it, then showed him a driver's license with her picture, a date of birth making her twenty-five human years rather than her five hundred.

"What the…, lady? You're a magician?"

She thought for a moment until she figured out what a magician did. "Yes, I can do magic."

He blew out a sharp breath. "Just wonderful."

"I think so." She smiled. "I much prefer it to violence."

His heart thumped in his chest. Cochran wasn't as immune to her as he tried to act. He didn't speak again until they reached her rented room at the hotel. Once inside, he turned to her. "I want to know why you now have identification but didn't in the alley. I also want to know why you don't give me straight answers to my questions. And…" He pointed at her. "How did you convince the chief—through a closed door, mind you—to let you go?"

"Please have a seat." She shed her jacket and hung it on a hanger before starting to peel off her tee-shirt.

"Whoa, now. That can be construed as bribing an officer." He leaped to his feet.

"You want proof. I have to remove my top clothing." She removed her shirt, her back facing him, and let her wings unfurl from under her skin.

Pierce

"This is not possible." He stared at the shimmering wings extending from porcelain skin. The room filled with the fragrance of flowers, and a blue aura framed Shayna. "Body-modification surgery?"

She shot him an exasperated glimpse over one fine shoulder. "They're real."

"Oh, right. Fairy." He smirked, glancing around the room for the air freshener. "They don't look strong enough to help you fly, but they're pretty."

She pressed her lips together and whirled around to face him, oblivious to the fact she wore nothing on top. "To use my wings, I must be small. To make myself small requires a lot of energy. This…not so much." She held her hands to her sides. Blue light shot from the tips of her fingers, and Pierce almost forgot he was alone in a room with a half-naked woman. Then, before he could open his mouth to say something snarky, she shot one of the rays at him and knocked him on his rear.

When he came to, she was wearing her black tee shirt, and he was lying on the bed. "You're telling the truth." How could it be possible?

"I am incapable of lying, at first anyway. Only those who follow the dark can lie easily."

He swung his legs over the side of the bed and rubbed the spot on his shoulder where her…whatever it was…had shot him. The spot throbbed. "Okay, I'm ready to listen now." He couldn't believe he'd said that. He had always prided himself on his steady thinking, and this scene was straight out of a fantasy movie.

"It will get easier."

"You can read my mind?"

"More like discern your feelings, but if I concentrate hard enough, then yes, I can read your mind." She sat in the chair across from him. "I will tell you why I am here if you will sit silent."

He nodded.

"Radella is a vampire controlled by a demon named Kasdeya. Deema is a fairy who has gone dark. They are three powerful beings, but I can beat them with your help. This is imperative."

Pierce bit his bottom lip. This had to be a dream. Stuff like this didn't happen.

"It's real, Detective."

"Pierce. My name is Pierce." After…whatever was happening, they might as well be on a first-name basis.

"Kasdaya wants control of your world and its people. She will turn everyone into her minions. I have been sent here to stop her."

"Alone?"

"With your help."

"Why me?"

"Because you have a pure heart, Pierce. You truly want to help your fellow humans."

He rested his elbows on his knees and put his head in his hands. His thoughts hadn't been pure a few minutes ago. "This is like a horror story. A dark fairy tale."

"Yes."

"Can you be killed, because I sure can."

"Yes, but I'd prefer not to tell you how." She laughed. "Of course, if a human were to kill one of us, a curse would spring back on them."

He longed to hear the musical sound of her voice again. Somehow, he'd make sure she laughed. "How did you find me?"

"I didn't. You found me. I went to the alley to

find Radella."

"There you go with half answers again."

She approached him and placed a hand on his shoulder. The burning from where she'd struck him immediately subsided and joy filled him.

"You showed up, I read your feelings, and chose you. Did I choose wisely?"

He stood. "I hope so. Man, wait until the guys hear more about you. We can trust the other detectives, once we prove you're for real."

"Let's not involve anyone else unless we have to. It isn't safe."

Great. Not safe, yet here he was being drawn into a battle with faeries, demons, and vampires. Just his luck.

3

Shayna

Shayna needed little sleep and woke before dawn. She stood in front of the window, coffee in hand—she found she really liked the humans' brew—and watched the city become active. Men and women in suits rushed here and there like sprites. People in ragged clothes held out their hands, making Shayna wish she could use her magic to help them.

She was on her third cup of coffee before a knock sounded on her door. Pierce. She smiled. With his handsomeness, he'd make a good fairy. She willed her heart to settle. Faeries and humans should not get involved. One of them always had a difficult, life-changing decision to make.

"Good morning," she said, opening the door.

Pierce brushed past her. "If you say so." His eyes narrowed. "How do we find these, uh, Radella and Deema? I know Radella manages a strip club—

"

"Fitting. She enjoys the lust her body produces in a man." Shayna held up her cup. "Marvelous drink. Want some?"

He blinked a few times, then shook his head. "No time for that." He took the cup from her and set it on the sideboard. "We need a plan."

"They'll come to us. In the meantime, we should strive to lessen the damage they'll do." Sadness filled Shayna. "The dark grows darker. Radella has called her people."

His face paled. "More vampires are coming?"

She nodded.

"Call your people."

"It is not time. I can only call when the Light is almost extinguished."

"You mean when you're almost dead?"

"Yes, but not all the way dead."

He rolled his eyes. "Why do I always get paired up with the whack jobs? Let's go see if Radella is working."

Shayna smiled. The atmosphere at the club would change drastically when she walked in. Only the downest of the down frequented such places so early in the day. Ignoring Pierce's questioning look, she strolled out the door. After he closed it, she stopped and raised her hands. Her palms glowed blue, and she placed them on the smooth wood.

"What are you doing?" Pierce leaned close.

"Guarding my room. Not even Deema will know this is where I sleep." She turned. "Shall we go?"

"Why don't you have pointed ears?" Pierce

walked by her side.

"Those are elves. We are not the same."

"Huh. So those are real, too. Can you make yourself small? Like fit-in-the-palm-of-my-hand small?"

She glanced around them, then spoke, "*Shreank*." She hovered in front of him until he held out his hand. She landed, leaned against his cupped fingers, and crossed her ankles.

He grinned. "This is convenient. I could hide you inside my jacket. If we didn't have work to do, I'd take you back to the room and see what other wonders you hold."

She reverted back to human size. "You'll see a whole lot before we're through." Not all of it amusing.

They drove to the club in the same car as last night and parked in the back. An alarming number of other vehicles crowded the lot. Things had escalated further than Shayna had thought. Time to spread a little light.

Pierce

No other word for it but ethereal. Before they entered the club, Shayna glowed with a white light. Faint, not blinding, but there.

All conversation stopped when they entered. Heads turned. The girls dancing on the raised platforms stopped their gyrations. He'd never seen anything so amazing. The averted eyes, the rounding of shoulders, the crossing of arms over nudity. Several patrons rushing from the building as if chased. Perhaps this…fairy…could help New York after all.

Shayna approached the bar. "We'd like to speak to Radella, please."

The bartender, a bald man standing well over six-feet tall and weighing at least two-fifty, took a step back. "Through that door."

Pierce stepped in front of Shayna and entered first. Radella, resplendent in black, grinned from behind a mahogany desk.

"Hello again, Detective." She peered around him, shrinking back a bit. "You must be Shayna. Turn off the light, will you? I'm not partial."

Shayna's bright gaze didn't falter, but she dimmed the glow around her. "Radella, I'm here to stop you and Kasdeya from taking this city."

The darker woman folded her hands on top of her desk. "Are you prepared to do that?" She asked with a sly smile. "My people are trickling into this city as we speak. Will you take them all on?"

"If I have to. Where is Deema?"

"How should I know? She comes and goes as she pleases in a flash of sparks. That woman loves to show off."

Pierce's gaze shot from one woman to the other. The tension in the room was palpable. The air crackled and emitted an aroma of flowers and ash. Surely he wasn't the only one to sense it.

Radella's attention shifted to him. "Do sit down, Detective, before you fall."

He complied, not because she told him to but because she was right. His legs trembled. He rubbed his eyes with the back of his hand. Even after what he'd seen with Shayna, it was too much to take in.

"Oh, look," Radella drawled. "He's overcome."

"Leave him alone." Shayna stepped closer to Pierce.

"Don't worry, little fairy, I won't harm him. He isn't my type."

Pierce couldn't help but wonder what her type was. "How many of you are coming?"

"Legions." Radella's smile widened. "More than one pretty little girl can handle."

"I doubt it." Shayna smiled for the first time since entering the room, bringing back the light. "I'm looking forward to ridding this city of darkness."

"Bring it on, sweet fairy." Radella showed her fangs.

Pierce shifted in his chair.

Shayna headed for the door, stopping once and glancing back over her shoulder. "It would be better if you backed off."

"That is something I cannot do."

Shayna gave a nod, then transferred her attention to Pierce. "There is nothing more to do here."

He stood, shot a sharp glare at the vampire, then followed Shayna. "Are you sure you can take on a legion of blood suckers?"

"There aren't a legion of them left. Maybe a hundred."

His heart stuttered. "You can fight that many

yourself?"

"With my armor on."

He scratched his head, wishing the surprises would stop. "Wouldn't it be better if you filled me in on what I need to know about all…this?"

"I will answer any questions you have. But right now, we need to find McRory's Pub."

"It isn't far." Full of questions, but not knowing which ones to ask, Pierce kept his mouth shut and decided to trust the pretty fairy with the long blond braid.

She strode ahead of him, slender and fit in tight black pants and that shiny blue jacket. He'd never seen anything like the fabric, or her. Was the jacket her armor? Didn't look like it could protect anyone, unless maybe protect a person from road rash if they had a motorcycle accident.

"The noise from your brain is making it hard for me to think." Shayna narrowed her eyes. "Do you ever let it rest?"

He opened his mouth, then snapped it shut and said, "Give me some slack. I'm being introduced to a whole lot of stuff I never knew existed other than in the pages of a book or in the movies. So, yeah, my brain is racing. Deal with it." He opened the passenger-side door.

She shrugged, clearly not put off by his snappiness. "Your world is new to me, too."

"You seem to be adjusting well."

She smiled, sending his heart somersaulting. "All the thoughts in your head are teaching me what things are called and used for. I'm adjusting more easily than you."

"Definitely," he muttered, closing her door and moving to the driver's side. He glanced back at the club to see Radella watching from the doorway. A vampire, and more of them coming. He needed to let the other NYPD officers know. Know what? No one would believe the city was about to be overrun by vampires and dark faeries. The idea was ludicrous.

"You cannot tell anyone," Shayna said as soon as he sat in his seat.

"Stop reading my mind." He turned the key in the ignition. "I have to tell someone. This city can't be caught unaware."

"I will send out a signal. The city will think they are fighting a war between gangs. Don't ruin their innocence to the darker world."

"You have the magic to tell an entire city how to think?" Scary.

"Not all at once. I'll have to visit each precinct. Fire Departments and hospitals, too."

His shoulders slumped. "We'd better get busy. Radella will feed again soon. She's been waiting two or three days. No more."

"While it pains my heart, you will not be able to stop her until all of them are stopped." She shifted in her seat. "Unless you know where she will kill next. Then, I can bind her."

"No idea. Can we set a trap?"

"Maybe, although it will be dangerous to the one acting as bait. Vampires move quickly."

"Hmm." Radella wasn't interested in him, and he hated to risk the life of an undercover detective. "I have to tell the other two detectives. They're the only ones who might be able to survive. We can tell them she's a suspect for murder, without too much detail." They wouldn't believe him anyway. But Radella was only one of a hundred according to Shayna. The task before them seemed impossible.

He cut a glance at the woman next to him. She didn't seem worried in the least. Resigned maybe, and more beautiful than any living creature had the right to be. He shook his head. Stop thinking. She reads your mind, remember? He groaned at the sight of a slight smile gracing her lips.

"Why the pub?"

"To speak with a leprechaun." She continued to stare out her window.

"Of course. I should have guessed."

4

Shayna

Shayna approached the red-haired man behind the bar, ignoring the sudden quiet of the early morning patrons at her presence. "Hello, Paddy."

He froze and circled around slowly. "I didn't do it."

She laughed. "Do what?"

"Whatever it is you're here to accuse me of." He resumed wiping a glass with a white cotton towel.

"I'm here for information." She perched on a black vinyl-topped stool and motioned for Pierce to do the same. "Not much gets past you and yours. I'm sure you're aware Radella, Deema, and Kasdeya are here."

"Who in our world doesn't know?" A scowl marred his ruddy face. "I don't want to attract their attention. Go away." He gestured toward the line of multi-colored liquor bottles gleaming like jewels under the overhead lights. "I've made a good life here."

Pierce leaned close, speaking softly. "What's he afraid of that you aren't?"

Shayna kept her gaze on Paddy. "The leprechauns are easily influenced, isn't that right?"

With a sigh, the red-haired man shrugged. "We've never caused the havoc these creatures of the dark are doing. We've not done more than cause mischief in this world."

"May I call on you to battle?"

He groaned. "I'll rally the troops, if it comes to that."

She placed her hands flat on the counter, the palms glowing a bright blue. "Don't betray me, Paddy. Don't try to leave."

His eyes widened. "I give my word."

"Is a leprechaun's word any good?" Pierce raised his eyebrows.

Paddy's scowl deepened. "Don't believe everything you read in fairy tales, Copper. If we say we'll do something, we will."

Shayna extinguished the blue glow. She'd gotten her point across. There wasn't a leprechaun around that didn't know the power of the Light. "Thank you." She smiled, pleased to see the the little man's tense expression soften.

"Aye. We love this world, too. If darkness takes over, we'll have to leave or succumb. Now, go. You're bad for business."

"Who else will help us?" Pierce asked the moment they stepped outside.

"The sprites said yes, the fae of the Light, the

police force, which I hope we won't have to use since they'll die in scores. I haven't asked the harpies yet."

"This is blowing my mind." He rubbed his hands roughly over his face.

"Some races we can't use. There is no way to make a winged horse fit into this world without your people seeing," she said over the top of his car.

He grinned and laughed. "I guess there wouldn't be. Where to now?"

"Wherever your dispatcher tells us."

"What?" His radio beeped. The dispatcher called all available officers to an abandoned warehouse. "How did you know?"

Shayna shrugged and got into the car. Pierce had a habit of asking questions even after knowing the powers she had. Why were humans so hard-headed? Yes, they grew up thinking magical creatures were nothing more than stories, but hadn't she proven everything was the opposite of what he'd once believed? She took a deep breath, letting it out slowly.

"I'm sorry." Pierce closed the driver side door. "Asking questions is a habit."

"Now you're reading my mind."

"I love it when you smile." Pierce started the car. "It makes me believe everything will be all right."

She wanted to assure him all would be well, but no lie could ever leave her lips unless there was no other alternative. Rather than give him false hope, she stared out the window as they sped toward their destination. More talk from the radio about violence and death. Her heart sank. Things were escalating too quickly. She needed to speak with Linette. "When we have a free moment, I need somewhere private. Preferably with trees."

"You're worried." Pierce cast her a sharp glance. "That scares me more than Radella."

"I don't want to frighten you, but things are dire. We may die fighting this battle."

"And if we do, all is lost."

She nodded. "But keep the faith, Pierce. We haven't lost yet. We are just beginning, gathering our forces. I've a plan."

"Care to let me in on it?"

"Not yet. Later." He wanted to know more. Curiosity filled his mind, swirling around the thoughts of what they would find in the warehouse. She knew not one but three bodies awaited them.

They pulled into a parking lot vacant of all but police vehicles. Ordered to wait for Pierce, they converged on him the moment he stepped from the car.

Detective Payson looked from Pierce to Shayna. "What's she doing here?"

Shayna thrust out her hand. "Undercover. Agent Sky."

He shook her hand. "Nice to meet you."

"Clever," Pierce said as the other man left. "You might want to use your Jedi mind trick on Detective Marshal, too. We'll be working with them a lot."

The other detective marched their way, shook hands with Shayna, thus securing her alias. "Three dead bodies. Homeless drug addicts from the look of things," he said. "Appears there was a struggle."

Shayna bit her bottom lip. Darkness filled the air with an oily slick. Radella was close, no doubt to watch the consequences of her dirty work. "Be careful. We aren't alone." Shayna headed for the building, Pierce on her heels.

"Who's here?"

"Radella."

"Alone?"

"I believe so. Tell your men to arm themselves. Bullets will not kill her, but they might make it not worth it for her to stick around."

"Guns at the ready!" Pierce pulled his weapon from his holster. "You need a gun, Shayna, in order to play the part."

She bent down, picked up a stick, and slyly turned it into a Glock. "Ready?"

Pierce

He really wanted to be able to do magic. Shayna could turn anything into anything with the blink of an eye, a wave of her hand. Not even the best close-up magician could best her skills.

She held up a hand, effectively halting the ten armed men behind her. "The assailant is inside. Keep your wits about you."

Pierce moved in front of her. She might be magic, he might be human, but his heart told him the world would fare better if he died and she lived. Without her magic, all hope was lost. He pushed open a steel door, wincing at the screech it made, and peered into a cavernous room. Three windows high on the wall provided enough light for him to see three naked bodies, two men, one woman, lying in the middle of the concrete floor. No sign of anyone else.

Using caution, he approached the bodies. All three had the tell-tale bite marks of a vampire, their skin pale from lack of blood.

"What in the name of all that is holy is going on?" Marshal peered around him.

"Gang initiation," Shayna explained.

The other men accepted her statement without argument. Magic had an effect on things, so far in a positive way.

A shadow in the corner of the room drew Pierce's attention. "Look out." The shadow darted at them, much too fast to be human. He'd like to see how Shayna would explain this phenomena. He stepped closer to his partners.

Radella, her long hair flying and high-pitched laughter chilled Pierce's blood. She lifted one uniformed officer and tossed him against the wall as if he weighed no more than an apple. He slid down the wall and landed in a heap on the damp concrete floor. Officer after stunned officer were tossed like discarded toys.

"Stop, Radella. Flee this place." Shayna's fingertips glowed with an unearthly light. She shot ray after ray from them as every man in the room opened fire with their handguns.

Radella stopped a few feet from them. The shooting halted.

Shayna aimed her hand. "Stop this—"

The vampire aimed a roundhouse kick at Shayna's head, missed and…vanished.

Shayna's duck prevented any contact. She turned to the group of confused men. "Cover your ears, Pierce."

He did, along with Marshal and Payson, who stood out of Shayna's sight.

"There is no one here but these three bodies," she said. "Shots were fired because we thought someone had fired at us first. In reality, it was the backfiring of an automobile outside." She motioned for Pierce to remove his hands.

"I thought you couldn't lie." He shook his head at his partners, letting them know to stay silent until he could speak to them in private.

Shayna narrowed her eyes. "Lying gets easier the longer I'm here, and I did say unless there was just cause. I'm not immune to human failings. This is a lie that had to be told." She glared at the other two men. "You'll regret knowing what you face in the future." She marched from the building leaving them to case the scene.

"I keep forgetting she can read my mind," he groaned.

Payson wiggled a finger between them. "You got some explaining to do. How can a human do that…whatever it was?"

"Hold that thought." Pierce assigned the duty of casing the scene to the uniformed officers, then pulled the other two men outside where Shayna waited, leaning against the car. "I'm sorry. I didn't tell them not to cover their ears. They heard you tell me to, but I think we can use them. My partners are good men, Shayna."

"What on God's green earth is going on?" Marshal crossed his arms. "Who, or what, are you?"

Shayna kept her beautiful face impassive for a few minutes before speaking. "I guess you'll believe more easily than Pierce, since you've seen a bit of it firsthand. My true identity must be kept a secret." She explained that she was a fairy, about the dangers filling their city, and what the world was up against.

Pity for his partners filled Pierce. Their angry expressions morphed from disbelief to shock to grudging acceptance. Kind of hard to deny what they'd just witnessed.

"You're telling us…" Payson rubbed between his eyes. "…that we are dealing with a demon and hundreds of vampires?"

"So far, yes." Sadness filled her eyes.

"Believe me," Pierce said, "it took me a while to believe her, too, but she has wings."

Shayna glanced at him as if he'd lost his mind. "I need to speak with my queen."

"Right. Private. Trees." He turned to his partners. "When your shift is over, come to my place. We'll answer any questions you have."

They nodded, then stood there as he and Shayna drove toward Central Park. He parked, amused as prostitutes and drug dealers scurried away the second Shayna stepped onto the sidewalk. Maybe they could solve all the world's problems by putting a fae of the Light in every city, country, and neighborhood in the world.

Shayna set off at a brisk pace, her bright blue gaze studying each tree she passed. Finding a dense clump of foliage, she stepped out of sight, leaving Pierce to follow. He wanted to ask where they were going, what she was searching for, but for once he let common sense prevail and kept his mouth shut. If she wanted to know his thoughts, all she had to do was get inside his head. It was nice having a partner who didn't talk all the time like Marshal.

They approached a large oak tree. Shayna waited, casting a stern look on a pair of homeless men who studied her with great interest but didn't leave.

Finally, one of them shrugged and got unsteadily to his feet. "Come on, man. We aren't wanted here." He gave Shayna a wink. "Good luck, my warrior."

She gave a slight smile and nod of the head. "Peace be with you."

"Who is that? Another mystical creature?" Pierce watched the two men leave.

"No. Only one of the few who recognize creatures of the Light when they are in their presence." She placed her hands on the tree trunk. A glimmering portal appeared. "Stay here," she ordered, then stepped through.

Without thinking, Pierce followed.

40

5

Shayna

Head after head turned as Shayna made her way toward the queen's chamber. No one spoke. Direct glares, narrowed eyes focused behind her…she spun around. Her blood chilled. "Oh, no."

Pierce gave her a lopsided grin. "You can't read my mind in here, can you?"

"You have no idea what you've done." Tears sprang to her eyes.

"What?" He glanced around them. "Wow, this is a beautiful place."

Shayna stiffened as the fae around them bowed. She whirled to see Linette marching toward them, expression grave, the members of her court walking proud behind her. Shayna bowed, grabbing Pierce's arm and forcing him to do the same. "My queen."

"Arise and follow me. Bring the human." The hem of Linette's robe brushed Shayna's leg as the queen turned.

Fear for Pierce clogged Shayna's throat. Why had he followed her? Couldn't the man follow simple instructions? She meant to keep him safe, but now his life lay in the hands of the queen.

Shayna led Pierce to the diamond throne room. "Don't say anything until she speaks," she hissed.

He nodded, eyes wide.

The chamber definitely took one's breath away. Prisms of color from the Light that never dimmed filtered through the diamonds. Thin veils of gold and silver ran across every flat surface. Linette sat on her gold-plated throne while the members of her court took their places behind her.

"Approach me, human."

Pierce cut Shayna a quick glance. She nodded and motioned for him to step forward.

"You, too, Shayna." Her voice sounded sad rather than angry.

Perhaps the punishment for Pierce entering their world would not be death as spelled out in the law. She stepped forward and bowed. "My queen."

Linette breathed sharply through her nose. "Did I not specifically instruct you not to bring a human back with you?"

"Yes, my queen." She kept her eyes focused on the stone floor.

"Your majesty." Pierce straightened. "This is my fault. Shayna told me to stay and I darted in after her without her knowledge."

Linette's eyes narrowed.

"My apologies," Shayna said. "I also told him to remain silent. The man refuses to do as I say." She shot him a cold glance.

"Leave us." Linette waved a hand dismissing her court. When they'd left, she said, "Arise, you two. We have more important things to discuss than whether this man should die or lose an eye."

"I could lose an eye?" Pierce paled.

"That worries you more than death?" Shayna raised her eyebrows.

Linette rapped her staff on the floor. "The darkness is growing. We don't have time for bickering." She focused on Pierce. "Your name."

"Pierce Cochran." He bowed his head.

"For Shayna, our best warrior and kindest heart, to have befriended you, you must be a good man."

"I try, ma'am."

"You obviously are now aware of the forces of darkness we face."

He nodded. "So are my partners."

Her attention whipped to Shayna.

Shayna sighed. "Humans are devious."

"Please exercise more caution, Shayna. We do not want to cause a worldwide panic in the human world."

"Again, my fault," Pierce said. "I truly didn't understand the rules of your world."

"Nor did you listen to Shayna, it seems." Linette quirked her lips. "She is a warrior. Listen to her. Let her take the lead. You will have to step down in your role as leader, Pierce. Just for now. If you would be so kind as to step outside, I'd like to speak to Shayna alone."

He nodded and cast Shayna a questioning glimpse before heading to the double doors. With a last glance back, he pushed them open and stepped out.

Linette's features hardened. "You are adopting some of the human vices. I know when you lie."

Shayna squared her shoulders. "It cannot be helped. In order to keep as few humans as possible from knowing the truth, I must convince them the destruction is caused by something other than it is."

"It saps a bit of your strength every time you lie. You must be careful. We are counting on you. Were you able to obtain help for when the time comes?"

"The leprechauns and sprites have agreed to help us."

"Visit the dragons. If you can get them to help before Radella does, we will be a formidable force."

Shayna's eyes widened. "We haven't used them for centuries."

"We haven't had a need. They, too, are dying off. This may be the very thing they need to thrive again. We must ward off the principalities of darkness with any means possible. Go now. Time is of the essence. Take your stubborn human friend with you. Get him some armor, and his partners."

"Really?"

"You need them."

Shayna wasted no time in joining Pierce. "We've a stop to make before we can head back to New York."

"Where?"

She smiled. "We're going to visit the dragons."

Pierce's knees gave out and he sagged against the wall. "No, flippin' way. Are they friendly?"

"We'll soon find out. But, first..." She flung open another set of doors. "Pick your armor."

"Wow." He ran his hands over finely knit steel in a rainbow of colors. "Do I wear this under my clothes?"

"Yes. Pick out some for the others." Shayna sat on a padded stool. "Quickly."

He chose armor in blue, green, and silver. "How do I carry these?"

She snapped her fingers and the armor disappeared. "They're waiting at your apartment."

"Is there any way I can become a fairy? I love your magic." His grin widened.

Ignoring a question she could not answer, Shayna rushed from the room leaving him to follow. Outside, she whistled for Crystal and swung onto the saddle. She held out her hand for Pierce. "Come on."

"Um, yeah, I don't like flying on the back of…anything."

She laughed. "How do you know? You've never done this. Come on."

He gripped her arm and climbed behind her, wrapping his arms around her waist, then Crystal soared into the sky. When they stopped near the portal, he slid off almost before Crystal's hooves touched the mossy ground. "Very cool and the most frightening thing I've ever done."

"Wait until you meet the dragons." She took his hand and led him into the portal.

Pierce

He must have been hit on the head a few days and now lay in a coma. Yes, he'd seen Shayna's magic, the destructive force of Radella, and he'd flown on a winged horse after visiting a fairy queen, but the surrealism kept him feeling as if he lived in a dream. Despite it all, he wanted nothing more than to walk the streets of New York where things were *real*.

Now, they maneuvered through a land piled with massive rocks, squeezing through crevices, on their way to visit a dragon. Pierce shook his head. Too *un*real.

With nothing but rocks to see, he feasted his eyes on the lovely sight of Shayna. The moment she'd stepped through the tree in Central Park she'd worn a filmy blue dress, almost transparent in its thinness. Her pale skin shimmered under the fabric. Her blond hair flowed over her shoulders. He glanced down at his serviceable dark suit. Maybe the faeries couldn't wear human clothing in their world.

He glanced at his watch. The hands had stopped at the time they'd stepped through. He sighed. After what he guessed was about an hour, they squeezed through a crack in the stones and into a wide, green meadow. The fragrance of poppy flowers almost overpowered his senses. He glanced at the sky, so blue it hurt his eyes.

Winged creatures flew overhead. The sun illuminated their glittering scales. One of them swooped down and landed with a thud in front of them. The ground shook under the dragon's weight.

Shayna bowed her head. "Gorna, we've come to enlist your aid."

The dragon replied in a language Pierce couldn't understand. Occasionally, it cast a yellow gaze on him. He took a few steps back from its glare.

"I need your agreement to help us fight the darkness in the human world," Shayna said. "With you by our side, we're sure to be victorious."

The dragon blew a spark from its nose, then glanced at the sky now teeming with dragons. If their species was dying off, there must have been myriads of them before. It returned its attention to Shayna.

"No, I cannot guarantee your safety, but having you there will make the odds better for us all."

Gorna said something else that sounded like a sigh.

Shayna nodded. "I look forward to hearing from you." She pivoted and headed back into the rocks.

"What did it say?" Pierce hurried to catch up with her.

"She said she would speak to the other elders and send a messenger with their answer."

"To my world?"

She glanced over her shoulder at him. "Of course. We don't have time to wait here for an answer. My skin crawls. Radella or Deema is up to something."

His stomach dropped to his feet. He prayed the dragons would answer the call for help. "Will all the worlds perish if the human world is destroyed?"

"No, but darkness will cover everything. Only

the creatures of the Light will be gone."

"What weapons can I use? My bullets will be useless."

"We'll have to make special ammunition for your guns. They'll have to be pure silver."

"Like for a werewolf?"

"A shapeshifter. They bleed like the dogs they are."

They covered the rest of the way in silence. Pierce didn't have to ask whether a shapeshifter followed the Light or the dark. Shayna's tone told him all he needed to know.

Eventually, they made their way to the portal, flew back to fairy land, and returned to Central Park. Shayna's clothing transformed back to form-fitting black pants and the shiny blue jacket.

"I preferred the gauzy dress," he told her, winking.

She rolled her eyes. "Let's meet up with your partners and hope they don't have heart attacks when I more fully explain what is happening around them."

Deema

Deema peered out the window of her renovated warehouse apartment at the New York Lights. Kasdeya had ordered her to stay put for her visit. A meeting to give orders, more likely. Sometimes,

Deema wondered whether the promised power and fortune would be worth the hassle of working with a demon. She sighed and drained the whiskey from her glass, wishing for at least the thousandth time that the liquid had the same effect on her as it did the humans. Instead, it tasted good to her palate, left a warm trail from her throat to her stomach, and little else.

"Why so morose?" Kasdeya materialized and sat in Deema's favorite leather chair. "A battle is approaching. One we are sure to win."

"Shayna is recruiting." Deema lowered herself to the sofa.

"Are you doubting what I'm saying?" Kasdeya frowned. "How can we lose? The harpies and shapeshifters are on our side, not to mention all that is left of Radella's people."

Deema shrugged. Shapeshifters were known for changing their mind if they thought the risk too great. They much preferred preying on humans they could transform into rather than fight those they couldn't change. "Just being cautious."

"Have you contacted the other dark faeries?"

"I've sent a messenger. They'll respond when they get around to it. You know they aren't as quick to please as the light fae."

Kasdeya laughed, the sound harsh and old. "Nobody is. How much nicer things would be if everyone just tended to themselves and stopped trying to force their ideas on those who believe differently." She pointed to the whiskey.

With a sigh, Deema rose and poured the demon a drink. She handed the crystal glass to Kasdeya and resumed looking out the window. The dark shapes of other demons flitted around the stars. So many of them it was a wonder the humans couldn't see. But, the smaller demons couldn't do much more than try and influence the weak-minded. Only the largest and strongest would fight in the coming battle.

She shuddered. Every time she found herself with more than one of them, her skin crawled.

"You aren't very good company tonight, Dee." Kasdeya plunked her empty glass on the table. "Sometimes, I think you're regretting our partnership. That would not be wise."

Deema stared into the demon's eyes. "I'm not having a change of heart."

Kasdeya laughed. "You have no heart. That's why we make such a good team."

The problem was…Deema did have a heart.

6

Shayna

Shayna fidgeted in her seat as she faced three detectives. It very much as if she were being grilled at a trial. Maybe she was. Pierce looked resigned, the other two curious with almost anticipatory expressions. Oh, why had Pierce put her in this position?

She took a deep breath. "What do you know, if anything?"

"Nothing," Marshal said, "that's the problem. Some weird voodoo sh…uh, stuff happened in that warehouse. Who was that dark woman?"

"Radella. She's a vampire."

Payson laughed. "Right, and I'm a werewolf."

"Not unless you've been bitten."

He glanced at Pierce. "She's serious?"

Pierce nodded. "You're going to need to suspend reality, forget everything you believe to be true, and listen. It took me a while to come to grips with her, but one zap of blue light from her finger convinced me."

"Show us." Marshal crossed his arms.

Shayna stood and held out her hands. Her palms turned blue. She turned and zapped the lamp off the end table.

Payson scratched his forehead. "What are you?"

"A fae of the Light. A warrior sent here to stop the coming darkness. Pierce, and now you two, will help me."

"Along with dragons, leprechauns, and sprites, don't forget." Pierce grinned.

"What are we up against, exactly?" Marshal rested his elbows on his knees and leaned forward.

"Vampires, demons, and a dark fae, to begin with." Shayna resumed her seat. So many questions whirled through the men's minds. "I know what you will ask, and I've told you what I can."

"Yeah, she reads our minds," Pierce said. "Be careful what you think."

The risqué thoughts in Marshal's mind dissipated so quickly Shayna couldn't hold in the laugh that escaped. She took no offense. Human men were such slaves to beautiful women. In the hands of one of the followers of the dark, they would be in grave danger.

"There is a great battle coming," she said. "One which I will lead against those who want to control your world."

"Why?" Marshal rubbed his hands down his face. "Why would the fairy world care?"

"We have always been closely connected with the human race. Your fate determines our own. If you fall, our light goes out."

"Like Tinkerbell?"

"Who?" She frowned.

Marshal shook his head. "Never mind. Now what?"

"Deaths will be escalating as Radella builds her strength. The stronger she gets, the stronger Kasdeya, the demon, gets."

"Radella is the manager at the strip club where we found the dead body a few days ago," Pierce added.

Both men's eyes widened. "Are all other world races as attractive as you two?"

Shayna smiled. "No. The harpies are quite homely."

"Good or bad?" Payson asked.

"Mostly bad, but some will join our side."

"So, there's no way of knowing who is human and who isn't, is there?" Marshal sighed.

"Not unless they reveal themselves to you in some way." Shayna stood and moved to the window. "Come see. I'll reveal the other world for you."

The three men crowded around her.

Shayna waved her hand and stepped back. "The flying shadows are demons causing disruption and influencing people's minds to do bad. Those on the ground with a dark aura around them are the vampires. The green are the leprechauns. That dark purple is Deema. Kasdeya, the demon working here, glows red."

"My God in heaven." Pierce glanced at her with wide eyes. "It's a kaleidoscope out there."

"I had no idea this was going on," Payson said. "I have to admit to being absolutely terrified. I wish I would have covered my ears and lived on in ignorance."

"The danger grows every day as more come to battle." Shayna closed the curtains. "Good and Evil have always battled for the minds of men, but that battle has increased recently. Thus the reason I am here."

Marshal swallowed hard. "How are we supposed to fight this?"

"Faith, and the skills I will teach you. All is not lost. There will be many battles before the last mighty one that determines your fate." Her heart ached for the fear in theirs. She wished she could take away the shadows in their hearts. Pierce held on to the faith that Shayna could save them. The other two didn't know what to think. She could only pray she would be the help they needed.

Shayna stared into the men's shocked faces. How could she train men to fight this type of battle?

Pierce

He studied the shocked faces of his partners, sharing in their horror and disbelief. Even knowing what Shayna was, having seen firsthand Radella's handiwork, Pierce still could hardly fathom the hundreds of dark shapes he'd seen outside Shayna's window. Too many to count. Too many to fight.

"When will the others come? Surely some of the good will come before you almost die."

Shayna shrugged. "The leprechauns will fight beside us. The sprites will wait. A few of the light fae, perhaps a dragon or two."

"Dragons?" Payson straightened in his chair. "We'll have dragons? How can we possibly lose?"

"They haven't answered yet," Pierce said, "but they are impressive."

"You've seen one?" Payson's eyes widened.

"Yes. I've been to the other world. Too beautiful to describe in words."

"Man, you have all the luck." Marshal slouched in his seat. "I want a fairy like Shayna and go to the other world."

"Maybe if you're a good boy," Pierce said, eyeing the bedroom door where Shayna had gone to rest.

"You like her," Marshal said.

"Of course. There's nothing bad in her."

"No, I mean like in a 'you're attracted to her kind' of like."

"Don't be ridiculous. We aren't in high school. Besides, we aren't of the same race."

"So? Some of the fairy tales we grew up on have to be real. Greek mythology. Gods and humans fell in love all the time."

"She isn't a god," Payson said.

"Quiet." Shayna stepped through the open bedroom door. "We aren't alone."

All three men jumped to their feet and removed their weapons. "Where?"

"Put those away." Shayna glared. "Those

weapons can't harm the undead."

Radella, Pierce thought. Or a demon.

A sword materialized in Shayna's hand. "Get behind me. There is only one."

A red-haired woman in scarlet leather appeared. "Put that silly thing away. I'm not here to fight."

"I'll keep it handy, if you don't mind, Kasdeya." Shayna kept the sword at the ready.

"You're the demon?" Marshal looked shocked. "Shouldn't you be ugly or something?"

"Aren't you cute?" she smirked. "I will be grotesque if the dark side loses. Which we will not." She glanced around the room. "May I sit?"

"No." Pierce stepped up to Shayna's side. "I'm pretty sure you aren't welcome here."

"How did you find us?" Shayna tensed.

"Oh, you lovely, naïve fairy. You might be able to hide your room from dark fae and vampires, but not from me. I'm too powerful." Despite Pierce saying no, Kasdeya sat gracefully on the sofa. "I must say, pretty fairy, that I'm surprised you revealed yourself to humans."

"What I do is none of your concern." Shayna's eyes brightened to an unearthly blue.

Kasdeya shrugged. "I've come to make you an offer."

Pierce narrowed his eyes. "Why?"

"Because, handsome, if she loses, you're all doomed. But if you side with me, you'll have more power and wealth than you've ever imagined."

"If you're trying to make a deal," Pierce said, "you must be worried about the outcome."

Her face darkened. "Do not toy with me." She

stood, fire flickering in her eyes.

Shayna stepped in front of him. "You will not harm him. These men are under my protection."

The light in the demon's eyes dimmed. She laughed and glanced at Marshal. "Some may not be as much." She snapped her fingers and disappeared.

"What did she mean?" Pierce glanced from Shayna to Marshal.

"Only that Marshal is not completely convinced he isn't dreaming."

"More like a nightmare." Marshal sat back down. "But I think I'm waking up." He shuddered. "She got inside me. I felt it, like a burning in my soul."

"You must fight the darkness, Marshal." Shayna put a hand on his shoulder. Her palm emitted a white light.

Within seconds Marshal's body released the tension. "Can she make me do things?"

Shayna shook her head. "Only influence. You must be strong to stand against her."

A cold hand gripped Pierce's heart. If his partners turned to the other side, he'd be the only man left standing beside Shayna. No matter how strong she was, he knew she couldn't stand alone against all those…things he'd seen outside.

"I think everyone needs to get some rest," he said. "Payson, Marshal, I'll see you at the precinct tomorrow and we'll formulate some kind of plan." Although he had no idea what.

"I doubt I'll sleep." Payson pushed to his feet. "My mind will be too busy processing this day."

"I can help you." Shayna reached out a hand.

He jerked back. "No thanks." He marched out the front door with Marshal on his heels.

"Don't worry." Pierce gave her a reassuring smile. "They'll come around."

"They have darkness in them. You shouldn't have let them know about me." She whirled and headed back into the bedroom.

Feeling like a young boy scolded by his teacher, Pierce left, closing the hotel room door behind him. She was wrong. Payson and Marshal were good men. He'd stake his life on it.

Shoving his hands in his pockets, Pierce headed for his car, glancing at the night sky. He couldn't see any of the creatures that flew around. None of the pedestrians around him seemed the least bit bothered. He almost agreed with Payson. Ignorance would have been bliss.

"Hello, detective." Radella leaned against his car. "I hear you had a visitor today."

"Go away." He took a step back.

"Do you taste as good as you look?"

He reached for his gun.

She laughed. "That won't hurt me."

He reached for a stake next to a newly planted sapling.

"Neither will that. Stop believing in fairy tales, Detective." She glided toward him.

Before Pierce could act, Shayna appeared in front of him in a shower of blue sparks, sword in hand. "You cannot have him."

Radella glowered. "Fine. I'll find me another boy toy. I wasn't going to kill him. Just make him immortal." She dashed away.

Shayna faced Pierce. "You're staying with me. Come on."

Saved again. He was becoming more of a hindrance than a help. "Why me?"

"Because you have something they think will tilt the battle in our favor."

"What?"

"I don't know yet."

Radella

"I'm starting to become disappointed in you." Kasdeya paced her penthouse.

"How does she always know when he's in danger?"

"She's formed a bond between him and her. You'll have to focus on someone else."

Radella pouted. "I wasn't going to kill him. I'd just like someone to spend eternity with."

Kasdeya made a sound of disgust deep in her throat. "Find someone else, although I have no idea why you would care. Binding yourself to someone closes off a lot of options."

"You think they've been intimate?" Her eyes widened. "Do the fae of the Light do that?"

"Don't be ridiculous. Of course, they do. Where do you think their infants come from? Sometimes I feel as if I'm working with children." Kasdeya rolled her eyes. "But, they most likely have more of a mental connection."

That went more along with what Radella knew of the fae. But, a mental connection was the first step toward a fairy-human bonding. If Shayna bound herself with the man, he'd be a lot stronger. Not fae strong, but stronger than any other human. Winning the battle might not be as easy as Kasdeya thought.

"What were the other two men like?" she asked.

"Handsome." Kasdeya grinned. "Not as pure of heart as Shayna's man. We might be able to influence them. I felt a great weakness in one of them when he looked upon me."

"I get the other one." Deema appeared in a shower of purple sparks and cast Radella a gleeful glance. "You'll have to keep looking, undead."

Radella glared. "When this is over, I'm going to kill you."

Deema smiled. "You can try."

7

Shayna

Shayna stood in front of her hotel window, sipping coffee as seemed her morning routine now. Her mind drifted to the day before and the fear on the faces of the detectives. She had no worries about Pierce following through with his offer to help, but the other two worried her. Not enough faith in either of them.

Outside the forces of darkness continued to accumulate. She shook her head. Today would be the first day of training for the three men. She prayed Payson and Marshal wouldn't use what she taught them to fight against the Light.

She headed for the door seconds before a knock sounded. She opened the door and stepped back to let the men in.

Marshal eyed the cup in her hand. "You drink coffee?"

"Of course." She frowned. "I have to eat and

drink, same as you."

His face darkened. "Sorry. You can't blame me if this is a bit too much to take in."

"Did you say we were training today?" Pierce glanced from his partner to Shayna.

"Yes. Are we ready?"

They nodded.

"Take each other's hand. You're about to experience something weirdly wonderful." Shayna smiled and grabbed a duffel bag from under the bed. She then joined her hands with theirs, closed her eyes, and transported three frightened humans to a clearing on top of a mountain in Asia.

"We won't be disturbed here." She set the bag on the ground as the men lost the contents of their stomachs. "My apologies. You get used to it after a couple of times."

Payson shook his head. "Absolutely not."

She glanced up at him. "Then how will you return?"

"What's in the bag?" Pierce asked, rinsing his mouth with water from a nearby stream.

"Armaments to use against those of the dark." She opened the bag and stepped back. The bag held human weapons modified to destroy what no mere weapon on earth could.

Pierce held up a sword with a silver tip. "So, I'm to stab them with a wooden sword?"

"The tip is silver. So is the sharpened edge. You can hold them at bay with the tip, but you have to bury the sword in their chests to kill them. Demons cannot be killed, but you can banish them with the holy water in the vials I've provided. Take up your swords, gentlemen."

"We'll kill each other." Payson stared at the broad sword in his hands.

"They are enchanted so you cannot harm any human with them. Have any of you fought with a sword before?" Shayna studied each of their apprehensive faces. "No? Swing the swords. Get familiar with their weight."

While they did, she strolled around them studying their lack of technique. None of them were horrible, but they weren't good either. "Spar with each other. Pierce, you're with me."

He adopted a fencing stance. "I'm ready."

She laughed, startling birds from a nearby tree. "This battle will be more like…what you would call street fighting. No rules." She swiped his legs out from under him with one sweep of her leg, then held her sword at his throat.

His eyes narrowed. "I'll never best you if you read my mind."

"Okay." She waved her hands over their heads creating a dome that enclosed the four of them under a protective shield. "No more mind reading."

"Good." He sprang to his feet and tackled her to the ground.

"You can't sit on a demon, Pierce. Skin-to-skin contact gives them the opportunity to get inside your head." She rolled over, now on the top and held his hands over his hhead. "You've got to stay an arm's length away, which will be difficult because they can fly."

He grinned. "But I like wrestling with you."

She playfully slapped his face. "Focus." She

shot up and swung her sword toward his head.

He rolled, sprang up with an agility that surprised her, and knocked her sword away from him. He advanced swing upon swing until he fought for breath.

Shayna parried every swing. "You're good, but you need to build up endurance. The three of you will jog three miles tomorrow, increasing that distance as the days pass."

Marshal and Payson, already winded, leaned against a tree. "Can't you give us something to make us stronger?" Marshal asked. "Surely you have something in your magical bag."

"And how are we supposed to walk down the street with a sword?" Payson fell to the grass.

"No one can see them unless their eyes have been opened to the other world." She wiggled her fingers at him. "Your turn to spar with me."

"Ugh." He lunged at her, his sword hacking the air.

She shoved him back. "You're clumsy. You'll die fighting like that." She advanced with a warrior cry, stopping her sword inches from his neck. "Again."

"You're brutal." Payson's chest heaved. "We need a break."

"All right. Fifteen minutes. There is water and food in the bag." Shayna sat on the thick grass and leaned back on her elbows. Her gaze searched the thick clump of trees on the other side of the dome. They weren't alone.

Deema

She wasn't so far removed from the other fae that she couldn't follow one of her kind. She'd been a follower of the Light once. A long time ago until a handsome dark fae lured her to his side. Now, he was dead, and she followed the whim of a demon.

She couldn't hear what Shayna and the men said but could tell from the grins on their faces they had a good time enjoying their lunch. Two of them sorely lacked fighting skills, but with Shayna as their teacher, they would be ready for any battle soon.

The dark-haired one, the one Shayna had connected with, held more skill than the others. Kasdeya would be thrilled with this information. If Deema chose to tell her. Kasdeya didn't have the mind-reading skill the fae had unless she touched the other person's skin. Any information Deema held back was hers alone. She rather liked the idea.

As she approached the dome, the four inside glanced her way. Deema couldn't enter without invitation, but maybe knowing she stood there watching would intimidate the men.

She smiled and flipped her hair over her shoulder, almost tempted to summon her armor. Had Shayna shown them yet what a fully armored faerie looked like? Talk about intimidation.

"Go away." Shayna's voice cut through the

dome.

"You can speak through this?" Deema frowned.

"I created it, didn't I?" She smirked. "What do you want? Ready to return to the Light? Our queen will welcome you if you truly desire to return."

"Not a chance. I've had enough of the simple life."

"You'd rather be at the beck and call of Kasdeya than live a life full of joy?" Shayna shook her head. "That is mystifying."

Deema growled and snapped her fingers to disappear.

Pierce

The dark-haired fae would be pretty if she didn't wear a perpetual scowl. He glanced at Shayna. Not the same type of beauty as the one with golden hair, but still lovely.

From the way the two fae stared at each other, they probably communicated without words. He sighed and took another gulp of water. As he stood, the dark fairy disappeared in a shower of purple sparks. "Let's get back to work. I have a feeling our skills might be tested soon."

"Your feeling would be correct," Shayna said, motioning for Marshal to spar with her this time.

Payson continued to gaze in the direction where the dark fairy had stood. "It's too bad she's on the wrong side. There's something about her that draws me."

"Come on. Grab your weapon. There's armor back at Pierce's apartment."

His face brightened. "We get armor?"

"Of course," Shayna said. "You can't go into battle without it."

When the men could take no more, Shayna transported them to his apartment and waited while they got sick again. He really hoped transporting was not going to be a regular occurrence.

After rinsing the foulness from his mouth, he flung open the closet door to reveal the armor. "Payson is blue, Marshal is green. I get the silver." He tossed the flimsy articles to each man.

"This doesn't look as if it would stop a penknife." Marshal held it up with two fingers.

"Do not be deceived by its weight." Shayna dropped to the sofa. "With fae magic and dragon scales, it will stop any blade. Hold them up and step into them. They will form to your body."

They did as told. Pierce ran his hands down the fine metal. He could hardly tell he wore anything. "What about our heads and faces?"

"Top shelf of your closet."

He pulled down helmets, gloves, and boots. "We're to wear all this under our clothes?"

"Every single day from here on out." She nodded. "No one will be able to see them but you."

Pierce sensed her frustration. Time after time she'd told him to trust her, and time after time, he doubted and asked questions. The woman had the patience of a saint.

"Who was the dark-haired woman?" Payson

asked, stripping to his underwear.

"Dude." Marshal frowned. "There's a woman present."

"Don't worry about her," Pierce said. "She thinks nothing of nudity."

The other two whirled to stare. "Mind giving us a show?" Marshal grinned.

Shayna rolled her eyes and kept silent.

Turning his back to her, Pierce disrobed, put on the pieces of armor, then his street clothes over that. The metal felt cool to his skin. Other than that, he wouldn't know it was there.

"I…we," he motioned to the others, "appreciate you taking this kind of care of us. I know I made your work harder by letting these two know about you, but it's better in numbers, right?"

She didn't appear convinced, but stared out the window instead of answering. He'd angered her the other day and didn't think she'd forgiven him. That hurt. He wanted her approval, a feeling that was foreign to him. He'd never cared much what anyone thought before.

He'd be a fool to fall for her. They came from different worlds, literally.

"This has been enough for today." Shayna stood. "Never take off the armor. You may shower in it. Pierce, pack a bag. I can't leave you here without me, and I've gained a fondness for the richness of my suite."

He nodded. "See you guys at her place at six a.m. for our run."

Payson sighed. "I forgot about that."

"We'll train every day," Shayna said. "You

must build up strength and skill. Run in the morning, do your normal routine during the day, and we'll train in the evening. Good night." She strolled out the door, leaving the men with their mouths open.

"Yep. I really regret not covering my ears." Marshal marched from the apartment.

"I agree," Payson said, following him.

Pierce did too. What would've happened if someone else had found Shayna leaning over the body outside the strip club where Radella worked?

8

Shayna

Shayna stared at the destruction that was once the club Radella managed. Nothing remained of the building or those inside but charred, still-smoking timbers. Tears welled in her eyes. She knew there were always casualties of war, but this was too many. Over a hundred at first count had perished in the fire.

"Any hope that Radella died in the fire?" Pierce stood at her side.

"She most likely set it to put us off her trail. All we can do now is follow the trail of victims she left." Shayna glanced up and down the street. For once, neither Radella or Deema were around to witness the aftermath. "There's a fight coming. It's too quiet."

"Let's look for survivors before that happens." Pierce moved closer to the rubble.

"I cannot go closer. There are iron beams."

"So?" He cocked his head.

"Iron keeps the faeries at bay." She hated telling even him of one of her few weaknesses. It would be too dangerous for too many to know.

He sighed. "I won't tell anyone. You're still stronger than I can ever hope to be. I'll do the digging." He retrieved a shovel and started pushing boards aside.

Keeping her distance, Shayna did a patrol of the surrounding area. Two sets of footprints were imprinted in the ground near where the accelerant was found. One sunk in several inches. Radella had a human helper. "Pierce."

He set the shovel down and joined her. "What did you find?"

"Radella didn't act alone."

"A big man, from the looks of it."

"The deep prints would be hers. Vampires weigh a lot more than humans, but it does look as if her helper is a man from the size of the other prints." This did not look good. Either the man helped her willingly or Radella was grooming him for an eternity of being a vampire. She told Pierce her concern.

"Get me a list of all male club workers, with photos," Pierce ordered one of the uniformed officers. "Now!" He turned back to Shayna. "We'll compare the list to the bodies, to those not working that day, and by process of elimination, we'll find her cohort."

Which would take time they didn't have. Pierce and his partners had been training for over a week. She hoped they were strong enough.

"Got one still alive over here," Payson called.

Shayna and Pierce rushed to the end of the alley. A man sat propped against the wall, his skin deathly pale, his chest still, but his eyes glared up at them showing he was still alive. Sort of.

"He's in the process of conversion. Look at his neck." She pointed out the telltale marks of a vampire bite.

"He's turning into a vampire?" Payson glanced up in horror. "What do we do with him? Stab him in the head like you would a zombie?"

"Zombies aren't real," Shayna said. "The only undead you'll encounter here are the vampires."

"Thank God for something."

"Hush." Pierce rubbed his chin. "There's no way to heal him?"

"He isn't breathing." Shayna narrowed her eyes. "He's already dead."

"We can't kill him in cold blood."

"He. Is. Dead. Fine, then wait for him to attack and call it self-defense." She whirled and stormed away. He had no idea what he was up against. Pierce would need to set aside his values when the darkness came. Humans were to be protected, but those who followed the darkness needed to be destroyed. She groaned and dashed back to the alley as the newly-turned vampire lunged toward Pierce.

Making her sword materialize in her hand, she stabbed the man through where his heart once beat. He crumbled to ashes. "That's how it is done." She brushed past the astonished detectives.

Pierce caught up with her. "Sometimes you scare me."

"You need to be more frightened." She whirled to face him. "You cannot hesitate. Hesitation will get you killed."

He pressed his lips together. "That man's shoes didn't fit either of the prints we found."

"No."

"So, are you telling me that Radella is flying around turning people into vampires?"

"Not flying. Vampires cannot fly anymore, but they are fast, and yes, that is exactly what she is doing."

"How do we stop her?"

"I need to find her and restrain or kill her." Shayna strode to the center of the sidewalk, closed her eyes, and lifted her face skyward. She shut out everything around her and focused on locating Radella.

Shadows swooped from the sky and surrounded her, clogging the air with evil and blocking her senses. Kasdeya's minions couldn't harm her, but their presence thickened the air around her, making it hard for Shayna to focus on any one thing.

"She's with Kasdeya." Deema's voice appeared in Shayna's mind. "You can't find her there."

"Where is she?"

"I can't tell you that. What I can tell you is that they will attack tonight to test the strength of the detectives. You've been warned" Deema's presence flittered away before Shayna could ask where the attack would come from and why the dark fairy willingly gave her information.

Taking a deep breath, Shayna approached Pierce. "An attack will come tonight. Finish up here so we can prepare." She leaned against the squad car, ignoring the curious looks of the uniformed officers and the pedestrians gathered on the other side of the yellow tape.

Half an hour later, the four sat in Shayna's hotel room. The three men sat stunned as she explained her conversation with Deema.

"So we sit here and wait?" Marshal asked, glancing at the window. "Shouldn't we close the curtains?"

"They cannot get to us here." Shayna handed the men bottles of water. "Keep hydrated."

"Then, we stay here all night," Payson said.

"Something will happen to draw us outside." A distraction the men couldn't ignore. Innocents would be in danger. That was the only way to make them leave the safety of her room.

Pierce

Fear clogged his throat. He wiped his sweaty palms down his pant legs over and over. Shayna had said their armor would protect them. The swords hanging on their backs, unseen by others, would be enough of a weapon. Doubt clouded his mind.

"Trust me," Shayna said softly. "This is not the great battle yet. It is only a test. You are prepared."

He nodded, feeling anything but prepared. Bending over, his folded hands dangling between his knees, Pierce fought to steady his breath. As the hours passed, a flicker of hope grew that it might be a false alarm.

Sirens wailed outside.

The three cell phones in the room rang.

Pierce glanced at his screen. The pediatric wing of the hospital was on fire. "This is it, guys." He met the worried gazes of his friends.

Shayna folded her arms across her chest, then quickly lowered them. She stood before them with her blond hair flowing over armor of such a bright blue it hurt his eyes. At first he marveled at her outfit covered in diamonds but realized the fabric was more likely made of dragon scales. Claws issued from her gloved hands. "Stay behind me at all times. Keep your backs protected. Stand in a circle, weapons at the ready."

Pierce wanted armor like hers. He also didn't want to be on the opposite end of her sword. Shayna had claimed to be a warrior. Now she looked like one. She held out her hands and they were transported to the parking lot of the burning hospital.

"Here is where we make our stand," she said. "The demons will be trying to prevent the firemen from doing their job. Our duty is to protect them."

"Not the kids?" he asked.

"The firemen. We protect them; they rescue the children. Do not break rank for anything." She held her sword at the ready. "We enter ahead of the firemen, surround them, and do whatever we can to keep them safe. Your armor will protect you from the flames."

"What are you doing here?" A fireman glanced

their way.

"Helping." Pierce forgot they'd appear as if they were dressed in street clothes.

"Don't get in our way." The fireman lowered his face mask and entered the building. A swarm of demons engulfed him the moment he stepped inside.

Shayna hacked away at them, her sword bouncing safely off the fireman's back.

Pierce gripped his sword and moved in to help as his partners turned their backs to his to form a fighting circle.

Three pale men in black marched down the hall toward them. With one swipe of his hand, the man in the middle sent the firemen flying into the wall where he crumbled into a heap.

Vampires.

Better three than a hundred, he thought, doing his best to remain positive. With a warrior cry, Shayna advanced at a faster speed than he'd ever seen her run before. Her sword slashed and thrust, pressing the vampires back inch by inch. Pierce rushed forward to help, giving his own war cry, rather pitiful in comparison, but it gave him courage.

Without hesitation his partners did the same, not breaking rank, still fighting as the horde of demons increased. "The holy water." Pierce dug into the pocket of his armor and withdrew the small crystal vial. Using his teeth, he uncorked it and splashed the water over the encroaching horde.

Payson and Marshal copied. Shrieking, the demons flew into the air and away from the hospital.

Pierce sprinkled the water on every fireman who passed and soon found his vial empty. They needed enough water to fill the fire truck's tank.

Shayna cast him a quick glance of approval and thrust her sword into a vampire's chest.

Once his partners caught on to sprinkling the firemen and took over, Pierce went to fight by Shayna's side. Minutes later, the three vampires were nothing more than piles of ash, blowing away on the slightest breeze, and Shayna led the three detectives from the hospital, carrying the unconscious fireman over her shoulder.

"How did you go in there without protective gear?" The fire chief frowned.

"We had some," Shayna said. "The fire is almost out." She laid the fireman on a gurney and pivoted toward Pierce and the others. "You did well." Her smile sent the shadows scurrying and made Pierce feel eleven feet tall.

"And you didn't have to tell a lie." He ran his hands over his armor. They wore the most protective gear created by any hands.

Radella

In slightly less than twenty-four hours, that blond wench wiped out four of Radella's men. They didn't have enough fighters as it was and were losing too many. She'd have to be quicker about converting, or Kasdeya would have her head on a stake. Radella shuddered. Nothing could be worse than spending eternity with her head on display.

She glanced at the large man sleeping in her bed. She'd brought the club bouncer, Dan, home for play, but his size would be an asset in the coming war, and she'd decided to keep him. Bending over him, she sank her teeth into his neck.

His eyes popped open, and he bucked under her. Still, he was no match for her strength. Stopping short of draining him dry, Radella straightened and wiped the back of her hand across her mouth. She'd tasted better, but only the good were sweet, and this man had a history of violence against women. If she could control that, he would be able to easily convert many women.

Satisfied, she sat in a black leather armchair and waited for him to convert. She didn't need sleep; soon he wouldn't either. The bed was strictly for the visitors she brought home instead of killing. Her heart might not beat, but she still had lusts that needed satisfying. Of course, one of those handsome detectives might be worth the risk of facing Shayna.

She shook her head. Maybe later if they weren't killed in the battle, she'd request all three of them for her playthings. When the battle was won, Kasdeya would grant her anything she desired.

The man on the bed woke and sat up. "Man, that was something."

She smiled. "Wasn't it, though?"

He put a hand to his chest. "I can't feel my heart."

"That's because you're dead."

Laughing, he shook his head. "Lady, you are no angel, and this room is not heaven."

"If I hadn't kept you in between heaven and hell, you would definitely have gone to hell upon dying." She moved over to him and ran a sculptured nail down his chest. "You're now a vampire like me. I control you." She captured his lips in a cold kiss. "Time to start your training so you can convert others."

"You're serious?" He ran his hands down his arms and legs. "My skin's cold. Why am I so pale?"

"You have no blood, fool. Aren't you listening?"

His gaze locked on hers. He cursed, calling her vile names.

She let him vent. There was nothing he could do to change the situation. Radella slapped his cheek a little too hard and resumed her seat to wait until he accepted his fate. She had accepted hers, and Shayna would also…someday.

9

Shayna

"I'd like to take you to dinner." Pierce's expression revealed a slight slipping of his confidence. "A break from…waiting for something to happen would be good for both of us."

Temptation flooded through Shayna with the force of a summer monsoon. It would be better to keep things on a business-partner level. Two warriors fighting for a common cause. But, the flicker of uncertainty in his eyes had her saying yes before she could stop the word from leaving her lips.

"What?" He frowned. "You don't have to. I'm not forcing you to eat with me."

"No, we need to eat."

"Then what is wrong?"

She opened her mouth, closed it, then said in a voice barely above a whisper. "It wouldn't do for us to be too friendly."

He laughed. "I'm not asking you to bed, Shayna. Just dinner."

Her eyes narrowed. His words said one thing, but the thoughts flittering through his mind were something altogether different. Still, he did think the same way she did. People of two different races were not meant to be together in that way. Once they did, a choice would have to be made; they'd be bonded for eternity. Shayna did not want to leave The Glen on a permanent basis, and she suspected Pierce loved his city as much as she loved her home.

"Do we need to go shopping?" Pierce asked. "Other than the flimsy thing you wore in your world, which I liked by the way, you haven't worn anything other than that jacket and pants."

"Don't worry. I'll be dressed appropriately." She'd need something fancy. He wanted to take her to a nice restaurant. "Give me thirty minutes. Do you need to change?" She eyed his suit.

"No." He sat in one of the easy chairs in her suite. "A suit is appropriate. It's not like I got dirty sitting around all day."

"I'm sorry you're bored."

"While I'm sitting here protected, the people of my city are in danger. The bad guys are killing, raping, and mugging the innocent. I'm in the safety of a hotel room with a warrior fairy." He tossed a wadded napkin at the trashcan and missed.

"Someone is in a bad mood." She reached out to touch him. "I can take those feelings away."

He pulled back. "None of that Jedi stuff. Let me sulk."

With a shrug, she said, "Suit yourself." She turned and closed the bathroom door behind her. Shayna understood his frustration. Perhaps Pierce was right. They would return to the streets tomorrow, keep their guard up, and work to ease the suffering of his people. Shayna was here to win a war, not start one. She had to wait until Kasdeya made her move and be on the alert for skirmishes set in her path to capitalize on her weaknesses.

After a shower, Shayna used magic to put her hair into a twist, then turned her jacket into a dress of the same brilliant blue. The dress hugged her curves and fell to just above her knees. In the human world, a brilliant hue of blue was her color and made her recognizable to other fae of the Light. Not only faeries but other magical creatures that followed the Light would know which side she walked with because of her aura. Those not of her clan could only see her aura if she revealed it to them. Thus the need to wear clothes of a certain hue. She applied a light covering of makeup and stepped out of the bathroom.

Pierce's eyes widened, and he leaped to his feet. "Wow. Just wow. I thought you were beautiful before, but now—you're, well, I can't express it in words."

She smiled. He didn't have to. She knew exactly how she appeared to him and couldn't help the warmth that filled her heart. Fae or human, females liked to be thought of as beautiful. "I'm dressed appropriately?"

"Woman, you'll have every eye in the restaurant on you. You're perfect." He gestured toward the door. "You might want to put some kind of shield over whatever it is that allows you to read my mind. Otherwise that pretty flush on your face might get darker as the night goes by." He winked and placed his hand on the small of her back.

Queen's mercy, he was right. She shut off that part of her senses before she became fully unclothed in his mind.

They took a cab downtown. Pierce remained silent during the drive, his attention on the world outside the vehicle's windows. As much as she was tempted to, Shayna didn't allow herself to read his mind and found she rather liked it. Staying out of his head let her feel more human.

"Where's your armor?" Pierce turned.

"Excuse me?"

"Well, I'm wearing mine. Is that awesome armor you wore at the fire under that dress? Because I don't see how it could be. That dress fits you like a fine glove." His eyes glittered under the passing streetlamps.

"Same as yours. Mine is naked to the human eye."

"Don't say naked." He grinned. "That sets my mind in dangerous territory."

Pierce

When Shayna had walked out of the bathroom in that dress, his heart stopped. Literally missed a beat. He'd never seen anything so beautiful in his twenty-eight years. "How old are you?" He whispered as they entered the restaurant. "In your years."

A slight smile graced her lips. "Three-hundred and ten."

His steps faltered, but his grin stayed in place. "You don't look a day over two-hundred."

She gave her magical laugh, the one he vowed to hear over and over.

Radella and a gargantuan man appeared from around the corner of the restaurant, and Shayna's laugh cut off. Pierce glared in the vampire's direction.

"Look, Dan. Aren't they a lovely mortal couple?"

The man's gaze locked on Shayna. "Delicious. I bet she's as sweet as cotton candy."

"Try it, undead, and spend eternity carrying your head." Shayna narrowed her eyes, then motioned for Pierce to follow. Man, he loved her grit.

Pierce ducked through the glass doors. "I thought cutting off the head killed a vampire."

"No, a silver-tipped stake through the heart kills them. Removing the head just leaves them headless." She cut him a sharp glance. "Do you remember nothing of your training?"

The hostess took a step back after hearing Shayna's statement, her face paling. "Table for two?"

"Yes, somewhere semi-private, please," Pierce said, resting his hand on Shayna's lower back.

Touching her left him feeling a spurt of joy, as if everything was fine in his world. A dangerous way of thinking with evil lurking around every corner, but he did like the feel of her.

The hostess led them to a small table near a window. "In the corner by a window." She offered a nervous smile and handed them each a menu. "If you need a cab later, let me know, and I'll make a call for you."

Pierce thanked her and pulled out Shayna's chair. He glanced up and met Radella's cold gaze from two tables over. Great.

"She won't attempt anything in here." Shayna unfolded her menu. "Besides, I can take on two vampires with one hand behind my back."

"I guess we know who her partner in setting the club fire is."

"Yes, I recognize that man as one of the bouncers." Shayna folded her menu. "What's filet?"

"A tasty piece of beef. Try it with a blue cheese crust. You'll love it." His world offered a lot of things he'd like to introduce her to. Her world probably held more than he could fathom. Magic. Who knew?

When the waitress arrived, Pierce ordered a bottle of red wine and placed their orders before turning to Shayna. "Are we going to have to fight tonight?"

She shrugged one shoulder. "It's quite possible."

"Then let's enjoy our dinner and worry about it later." He reached across the table and took her hand. "Let's pretend we're just a normal couple on a date."

"Date?"

"Going out to get to know each other." So, she still wasn't reading his mind. He entertained some thoughts that would definitely make her blush. Once Radella and her goon confronted them, he felt certain Shayna would lift whatever block she'd put on. By doing so, she could work better with him and not have the two of them tripping over each other during battle.

"Let's get to know each other," he suggested. "We might be working together for a long time." When she nodded, he continued, "How long do the fae live?"

"Depends on which race. The dragons live the longest, sometimes centuries. My people live well into the hundreds. I'm still young in my world."

"Are you aging faster being here?"

"No." She smiled. "I'd age faster if I was half human, but I'm not."

"So humans and fae do mingle."

"Yes, although it isn't wise."

"Why?"

The look on her face told him that strand of conversation was over. "My turn. Why did you choose your occupation?"

"My father was a cop and his father before him. It's a trait in our Irish family."

"Any leprechauns in your bloodline? A lot of the Irish do have some."

He laughed and leaned back against the seat. "Seriously?"

"Yes." She tilted her head.

"I have no idea. How would I know?"

She thought for a moment. "Stand between me and the other diners and give me your hand. It wouldn't be wise to let anyone see. Shocking the hostess with our earlier conversation was enough for tonight."

He followed her orders and placed his hand in hers. She laid a glowing-green palm flat on his. Heat radiated up his arm and his own hand turned a light shade of emerald. "Whoa."

"You definitely have leprechaun blood. Someone in your family joined with a fae."

He lowered himself into his seat, his hand still tingling. "What does that mean for me?"

"My queen must have suspected. It is not common to let a crime such as entering our realm uninvited go unpunished, but with you having fae blood, she would have considered you one of us." She smiled as the waitress set their plates in front of them. "Smells delicious."

"Let me know if I can do anything else for you." The woman moved to another table.

"So, am I magical or anything?" He really hoped he could learn something.

"The leprechauns aren't like some of the other fae, but it's possible. Did your family ever suffer financial loss?"

He shook his head. "We inherited some land in upstate New York and some stocks. I've always considered us somewhat well-off. We also age well."

"There you go."

She seemed pleased, but Pierce was still

confused. "So, we can't do magic, but we have money?"

"Your ancestor would have made the gold. It's possible you could if you were trained. Oh, and you might be able to teleport. You could learn some magical tricks of self-defense if taught properly."

He doubted about teleporting, although the last time Shayna had transported them to the mountaintop in Asia, he hadn't thrown up. "Maybe I can talk with that bartender when this is all over or you can teach me."

"It would be a good place to learn more. Let me think on what you might be capable of."

He thought back to photos of his great-grandfather and the brilliant red hair that some of his family had. Pierce had taken after the female side of the family in his coloring with dark hair and blue eyes. The red hair must come from the leprechaun side.

He flipped his hand over and stared at his palms. No longer green and back to normal. Wait until he told Payson and Marshal he had a bit of magic in his blood.

After they finished eating, they had the hostess call them a cab and stepped outside to wait for their ride. "Stay close," Shayna said, stepping closer to his side, her back stiff.

"We aren't going to make it to the cab, are we?" She shook her head, and his blood ran cold. "Where?"

"Across the street in the alley."

"With all these people around? There'll be casualties."

Shayna closed her eyes, her lips moving as she chanted something. She held her hands above her head, her palms facing the sky. A white haze lowered over them, enclosing the street and sidewalks they and the vampires stood on. "We're invisible to the others now." She crossed her arms, jerked them downward, and changed to her armor.

Pierce changed in a much duller way. He pressed a button on the watch that had come with the protective clothing, and his street clothes disappeared. He pulled his sword from its scabbard as he and Shayna advanced.

Radella

"They're eating at a restaurant?" Kasdeya's eyes widened. "As if everything were normal?"

Radella ordered Dan to pour three whiskies and took a seat across from the demon. "Yes, Dan and I entered and watched them until you summoned me." They would have had to leave soon anyway. The manager had sent hard looks their way when they ordered nothing to eat.

Kasdeya paced in front of her large window, then stopped and gazed out over the night sky. "Look how dark it has grown."

"Looks promising." The demon wasn't talking about the fall of night, but the increasing number of those who followed the dark. The sky teemed with them. Every vampire Radella had under her command now roamed the streets doing their best to convert more. Something that grew increasingly difficult as the city called in more law enforcement. There just weren't enough undead to outnumber them. If they waited long enough, Shayna would find a way to outfit every officer with silver bullets, and the battle would be lost before it began.

Dan brought their drinks and hunched in a leather chair. "I want that blonde."

Radella rolled her eyes. "Down, big boy."

"Why did you convert him anyway?" Kasdeya pushed away from the window. "He doesn't seem very bright to me."

"Hey." Dan scowled and sprang to his feet.

"Sit down. You're no match for her, you idiot." Radella glared. "I converted him for his size and strength, not his intelligence."

Kasdeya didn't look convinced, but shrugged. "I'd think you'd be pickier when your numbers are so few. Send a few of your people to try and take down that detective. He's stronger than he, or we, know."

"It won't be easy with Shayna hovering over him twenty-four seven."

"If you keep at it, day after day, you'll wear them down."

She didn't think so, but Kasdeya was the boss. She sent out mind waves to the three vampires closest to the restaurant and gave them Shayna's and the man's descriptions. "Do not kill. Bring them alive." She didn't care what Kasdeya said. Radella wanted the detective for herself.

92

10

Shayna

Shayna held up her hands and shot laser after laser at the approaching vampires, which did nothing more than slow them down and piss them off. They glanced at each other and charged with a speed that frightened even her. "Keep your back to me, Pierce. They'll surround us."

"Can we take them?" His back brushed against hers.

"Of course."

"And there are no demons."

She smiled and gripped her sword. "You're right, and no one new can get through this shield. Let's fight." She screamed her war cry and met the vampires in a clang of steel against steel. So, someone had armed the bloodsuckers. Interesting. Kasdeya must be more worried than she let on.

These two male and one female vampires were stronger than the first three. The woman charged straight for Pierce while the men tried to separate Shayna from him. One of them held an iron bar in his right fist and stretched his arm toward her.

Pierce whirled and knocked the bar from his hand. He tossed Shayna a wink and spun back to fight the female.

Using her sword, Shayna pushed the rod away and then lunged forward, her weapon piercing the chest of one of her attackers. The other screamed and leaped into the air, knocking her off her feet. Shayna slid across the asphalt, rolling to avoid him pinning her down, then kicked out her legs to knock him to the concrete. A hard thrust of her sword into his chest finished him off.

She unwound the silver chain from her belt and whipped it through the air. It twisted around the female, holding her into place. Shayna faced her. "Who gave you weapons?"

The vampire's hard gaze seemed to bore through her.

"I'll finish you off if you don't tell me."

"You'll finish me off anyway." Her lips curled into a smirk. "I will not help you best the dark."

"You've been converted for a long time." The evil rolled off her in waves.

"Over five hundred years."

Then there was no saving the woman, not even to be used as a slave to the dragons. Too much darkness for way too long. Shayna sighed and turned her to ashes with one thrust of her sword, then hooked the silver rope back on her belt. She glanced up and met Pierce's gaze.

His chest heaved as he struggled to gain control

of his breathing. "That was intense."

"You did well." She cupped his cheek. "Let's go to the room and teach you some magic."

"Sounds good."

She removed the shield. Once again in their fine clothes, they waited on the sidewalk for a cab as if nothing were amiss. The vampires hadn't seemed intent on destruction. The iron bar led Shayna to believe they wanted to capture rather than kill. She glanced at Pierce.

The thoughts whirling through his mind filled her with sadness. Doubt and fear almost consumed him at times. With how hard it had been to win over three vampires, he feared they wouldn't be able to win when confronted with hundreds of them. That didn't include the demons or shape-shifters. Shayna prayed the shape-shifters who mostly remained neutral would continue not to choose sides.

She slipped her hand in Pierce's. "We will win this war."

"I wish I had your faith." He gave her hand a squeeze.

"You have enough."

A cab pulled up to the curb, and Pierce opened the back door for her. She slid in, enjoying the gentlemanly gesture. The moment the driver stared at her through the rearview mirror, her senses went on high alert. She kicked Pierce out of the car and slammed the door a second before the cab peeled away from the curb.

A glimpse back showed Pierce bolting to his feet and giving chase. It wasn't humanly possible for him to catch them.

"Who are you?" She focused her attention back to the driver.

"A human who knows which side to fight on."

She reached her hand and brushed his shoulder. The man had no magical powers. He truly was only a human, brainwashed into kidnapping.

"Who were you after? Me or him?"

"Him, but I suspect you'll do."

"Do you know what I am?"

He narrowed his eyes in the mirror. "Just some woman I was paid to grab. Well, you pushed the one I was sent to get out of the car. My employer won't be happy."

"No, I don't think they will." She leaned over and placed her hand more firmly on his shoulder. "You'll be fine, sir. Please take me back to pick up my friend."

"Of course." His hard-toned arm softened at her touch. Good. Further proof he was only human.

They stopped where an angry Pierce waited. "Do not ever do that again," he said, climbing into the car.

"My job is to protect you. I needed to assess the situation. All is fine." She tugged the hem of her dress down. "Are you injured?"

"A few bruises." His posture didn't lessen its stiffness.

"I will care for those when we reach the hotel and I explain what I know."

"And I'm supposed to be the obedient mortal and sit quietly." He crossed his arms and stared out the window.

"Yes. Do not forget I am the leader here. I will

protect you at any cost, but I will always do what I think is the right move. Pouting will not change that." Sometimes humans acted like children.

"I'm not pouting."

"Then stop sulking."

"Why are you so intent on keeping me safe over anyone else?"

How could she explain how she felt about him? How she'd vowed to make sure he didn't perish? Shayna might not be able to bond with him, but that didn't mean she wanted him to die. The very opposite in fact. She'd made a vow, and Shayna always kept her vows.

She glared out her window as Pierce continued to grumble. The man was impossible. Her fingers tingled with the temptation to zap him with a happy laser.

They continued the ride in silence, including the trip in the elevator and the walk to her room. Shayna rolled her eyes and entered, leaving Pierce to continue his sulk while she changed. When she joined him again, he glanced up.

"Do fae not have emotions?" He asked. "Can you not understand how I feel?"

"I understand perfectly, Pierce, but I—"

"Have a job to do. I know." He ran his hands through his hair. "I don't want to learn anything more tonight. I'm tired and bruised." He loosened his tie, then removed it. "I'm sleeping in the bed. Either join me or curl up somewhere else. I've had enough of the chair." He stripped to his underclothes and slid under the sheet.

Shayna's mouth opened. He'd always slept in

the chair. Pierce must be angrier than she'd thought. Disrobing, she climbed into the other side of the bed and fell asleep to the sound of his soft snores.

Pierce

Pierce woke the next morning and found himself face-to-face with a beautiful, sleeping Shayna. He shifted position and immediately regretted his surly behavior the night before and his refusal to let her take away his pains.

He lay there, his gaze roaming over the soft curve of her cheek, her full lips, the slight cleft in her chin. Sheer beauty to his eyes. Then, her amazing eyes opened, and her lips curled. He couldn't help himself. Before she had the chance to read his mind, he kissed her. All his fears melted away as warmth coursed through his veins. "I've kissed girls before, but wow."

She sat up. "That cannot happen, Pierce."

"So it wasn't a good kiss to you?"

She shook her head. "It was wonderful, but I'm fae, and you're—"

"A little bit fae. Isn't that enough?" He propped himself on one elbow. "Look at me, Shayna."

She slowly lifted her gaze.

"Do we really have to worry about anything more than now? Can't we enjoy each other, give a little comfort…"

"No. Fae cannot act that way." She got out of

bed. "Get up. I'll order room service, and we'll commence with your training. The other two will be here later, and I'd like to teach you some magic before they arrive."

"Yes, boss." He groaned and flopped onto his back. She was probably right. A physical relationship would distract them both from the task at hand. He threw aside the blanket and rose to get dressed, putting on the same suit he'd worn the day before. Like he'd said, it didn't get dirty sitting around the hotel.

Twenty minutes later, room service delivered two omelets, two orange juices, and a fresh carafe of coffee. Shayna would be pleased with more coffee.

"Food's here," he called.

"Just a minute." A few minutes later, she joined him, looking pleased. "I spoke with my queen, and she gave me some insight into what you might be able to learn."

He started to ask how she'd spoken with the other woman but decided against it. Fae like Shayna could do a lot he'd never understand. "I'm excited. Can I shoot lasers from my fingers?"

"No," she chuckled, "but there are a couple of offensive moves you might master in addition to defense. First, you need to harness your magic. Focus on where I touched your hand last night. Summon the green."

"Really?" He stared at his hand. "Just concentrate hard enough?"

"Yes, it'll get easier over time." She poured the two of them coffee.

He concentrated until sweat broke out on his forehead. Finally, a green circle the size of a quarter appeared. "I did it." He grinned.

"You'll need to do that before each act of magic," she said as the spot started to fade. "Keep the green showing while you do magic. Now, turn the egg green."

"How will that help in a fight?"

"I need to see how much you can do."

He held the green dot over the omelet and willed it to turn. It morphed into an unappetizing color. He frowned and moved his hand. The cover to Shayna's plate flew across the room.

"Now that was cool!" He waved his hand toward the lamp, sending it crashing to the floor. "I can move things."

"I was not expecting that." She returned his smile. "You may have more fae in you than we thought. You'll need to learn to control your magic."

"What else can I do?"

She pulled a silver knife from her boot. "Make that fly and stick into the wall between the bed and the bathroom."

Now that he wanted something to fly, he found it harder to do. "What happened?"

"You can do it. The other came naturally. This will too." She started eating her omelet as if humans threw things all the time using nothing but a wave of their hand.

As for Pierce…he could do this all day. Finally, he directed knife after knife to go exactly where he wanted. "When can I get my own silver knives?"

"I'll have some delivered within the hour. Eat." Her eyes sparkled as if she held a secret.

He longed to kiss her again, but not wanting one of the knives sticking in his gut, he nibbled on a piece of toast. "Can I show the guys when we head to the mountain?"

"Sure. What's one more unbelievable thing?" She laughed and poured herself another cup of coffee. "I wonder if I can take this drink back with me when I return home. We don't have coffee in The Glen."

Just like that all the good feelings inside him vanished at the thought of her leaving. From the pained expression on her face, she knew what he thought. Could she possibly feel the same?

Her lashes lowered to hide her face as she lifted the mug to her lips.

Pierce wasn't adverse to following the rules; he did so every day, but some were meant to be broken. Their remaining apart, not allowed to explore the emerging feelings between them, was definitely a rule that needed breaking.

"Hey, coffee!" Payson slammed open the door. "I hope there's more."

Shayna nodded. "Help yourself. There's some in the pot on the sideboard if we run out here."

The pot on the sideboard immediately filled with coffee. Pierce shook his head. He couldn't do all that Shayna could, but moving things with a wave of his hand was mind-boggling. He turned his palm green and caused the cup Payson reached for to slide away from him.

"What the heck?" He reached for the cup again,

only to have it move. "Stop it, Shayna."

Marshal's eyes widened. "It's Cochran doing it. She gave you magic?"

"Nope." Pierce leaned back in his chair. "It appears I have some leprechaun in me."

"Some people have all the luck," Payson said, gripping the cup. "How did you find that out?"

"Shayna held my hand."

Marshal held out his hand. "Check me."

Shayna laughed and turned her palm several different colors before stopping. "No, you are one hundred-percent human." So was Payson, it seemed.

"Like I said, some people have all the luck." Payson sat at the round table near the window. "Are we ready?"

Pierce shook his head and reached for a piece of toast. "I'm waiting for my knives to arrive."

Marshal cursed. "Can't we at least be taught some kind of magic?"

"I'm sorry." Shayna looked apologetic, as if she could do anything about their DNA. She set her cup on the table. "We do have something to discuss. Last night, a human man tried to kidnap Pierce. A cabdriver."

"Why me? It was you he took." Pierce added cream to his coffee.

"It was you they were after. He didn't know why. I cast a spell to rid him of the darkness, at least temporarily. That's why we came back for you. If Kasdeya is influencing humans that quickly, things are worse than I thought. We cannot trust anyone outside of this room."

"Maybe he already packed a demon," Payson said. "Like he was possessed, right?"

"It's possible. Those without the Light can be possessed, yes. He said someone paid him. That's a big influence for any mortal without the Light."

"Not for me." Pierce held up a gold spoon. "Look what I just did."

Marshal sighed. "Good. Give me a pot of gold to pay off my mortgage."

Pierce tossed him the spoon. "Merry Christmas."

"Let's go, gentlemen. We've work to do. One hour on the mountain, then the rest of the day doing whatever detectives do." Shayna stood. "We've got to protect as many people as possible. Not only will Pierce be receiving his silver knives, but you both will have silver bullets and daggers. I'm in the process of having silver bullets delivered to every precinct and law enforcement in the city. They'll think them normal ammunition with an order from their chiefs to use the new ammo." She met each of their gazes one at a time. "Things are getting serious."

Before Pierce could ask her to explain, his cell phone buzzed. "We've another vampire death, guys." So much for further training. That day at least.

11

Shayna

Not only one, but three. Shayna put her hands on her knees and pushed to her feet. Why kill in threes? There had to be some significance.

She glanced around the vacant building. Two young men, both strung out on drugs, watched with bleary eyes from a far wall. They'd stumbled upon the bodies while searching for a place to snort their white powder. Shayna would never understand the activities some humans enjoyed.

Kasdeya tested the weakness of Shayna and the detectives every day now. It would continue to grow until she found the point they started to break, lose faith. Then, she'd attack in full force. If that happened anytime soon, Shayna and her human friends would fall. Shayna would have failed to protect them and her people. The idea dried her mouth.

Again she surveilled the building. At the last

kill, Radella had been watching. Shayna could not show any weakness. She narrowed her eyes as a shadow moved, and Deema stepped into the light. Shayna raised her palms.

"Hold on," Deema said. "I'm not here to fight."

"Then why are you here?"

Deema glanced at Payson. "I can't do this. I need you to help me come back to my first people."

"I have ways of knowing whether you're telling the truth." Shayna kept her palms facing outward. "It will not be pain free. You know the test you'll have to take."

"I know. Take me back." Deema's eyes shimmered. "If I continue along this path, I'm dead. Already hope is abandoning me."

Shayna shot a bolt of blue, catching the fae in the chest. Deema crumpled to the ground.

"She was surrendering." Payson knelt next to Deema.

Shayna yanked him to his feet and tossed him aside. She didn't like the act of capturing her once-upon-a-time best friend, but Deema would certainly die if it were discovered she gave herself up. "Stand back, human."

Payson's face reddened. He took a step toward her until Pierce stopped him. "She knows what she's doing."

Casting a grateful glance Pierce's way, Shayna seized Deema's hand and disappeared with a shower of blue and purple sparks. Once they landed near the portal, she slung Deema over her shoulder and entered the fairy realm.

Heads turned and voices silenced as Shayna

strode toward the queen's throne room. As she approached, her booted feet thudding on the marble floor, a guard swung the double doors opened and Shayna dropped Deema at the queen's feet. She bowed. "May I speak to you in private?"

Queen Linette waved a hand in dismissal and those in attendance left the room, closing the doors behind them. "You've captured Deema. Very good."

"She surrendered. For her safety, I made it look as if I captured her." Shayna straightened.

Deema groaned and sat up. "You were a bit too rough for my taste."

"Do not speak unless I command you." The queen stepped from her throne and approached them, her gown flowing around her crystal-shod feet. "Why surrender? I thought you craved power above all else."

Deema lowered her gaze. "I did, but Kasdeya is murdering humans on a whim. It's only a matter of time until I'm commanded to do the same as Radella, or worse, convert. It seems I'm not as hardened as I thought."

The queen met Shayna's gaze. "Do you believe her?"

Shayna shrugged. "There is a sure way of finding out, my queen."

"An unpleasant way, but sure." Queen Linette snapped her fingers. "Arise, Deema." The queen cast a spell that entwined Deema's wrists with a silk rope. "Shayna will take you to the den. If she is satisfied at the conclusion of your testing that you truly want to rejoin the Light, we will discuss how you can most help us. We do not turn away any who truly desire to join us."

Shayna gripped Deema's elbow and helped her to her feet. The unpleasant task ahead of her left a metallic taste in her mouth. Her friend was not the first fae to be tested, but it was not something to be enjoyed by the one doing the testing. Still, the safety of her people depended on Deema being truthful about her change of heart.

The den was an icy room filled with darkness. Shayna illuminated the room with a tiny ball of light that shone two feet in front of her. The only object in the room was a single chair made of carved stone. She placed Deema on the seat and secured her to the chair. With a sigh, she knelt in front of her. "Are you sure?"

Tears welled in Deema's eyes. "Yes."

"Then you must be made clean again." Shayna stepped back and extinguished the light. Thunder rumbled overhead. Lightning slashed. An icy rain fell over the chair where Deema sat. Isolation, cold, and the electric shock of the lightning would cause Deema to break if she were sent there under false pretenses. If she could endure that storm that would only increase in velocity, and what came next, she would be proven innocent and welcomed back into The Glen.

Deema sat silent for two hours. Shayna moved on to the second test. She opened a gate in the wall and released the captured demons. The clattering sound of their chains added to the rumble of thunder. She hoped Deema could withstand the torment they would do to her and not give in. This would be her final test.

"Hold strong." Shayna's voice boomed across the room. "You were easily influenced once. Don't make the same mistake again."

She left the room as Deema shrieked in pain. Her heart wept at the pain she'd only heard about that fae received in the den.

The next morning, Shayna led a subdued Deema back to the queen's throne room. This time unbound and walking of her own accord.

Queen Linette smiled as they entered the room. "She did not influence this time."

"No, my queen. She stood firm." Pride for her friend filled her.

"Look at me, Deema." Queen Linette kept a tender smile on her face. "I have a job only you can do. It will be dangerous. Are you willing?"

"Yes, my queen." Deema raised her gaze. "Anything."

"I will put a protection over you, so Kasdeya and Radella will be none the wiser as to what you've gone through. I need you to go back and relay information to Shayna about what the dark side does. This is something that is sure to turn the battle in our favor."

"I am willing." Deema flung her dark hair back from her face. "Even if it results in my death."

"Let's pray it doesn't come to that. You must return on your own. You cannot be seen in Shayna's company."

Deema nodded and turned to grip Shayna's hands. "Thank you, my friend. You saved me."

Tears spilled down Shayna's cheeks. "We will

fight side by side one day. We will win this war against evil."

"How will I have escaped? Everyone knows it is impossible to escape the realm once bound."

"A shifter attacked in the park. You escaped while I fought a great wolf." Shayna could find one easily enough and leave the body as verification." She glanced at the queen and received a nod of confirmation. "Give me an hour before making yourself known to Kasdeya." She released the other woman's hands and sprinted for Crystal.

Less than an hour later, having bought a wolf from the dragons by paying a handsome price for taking their supper, Shayna lay the dead shifter in the center of a clearing. Ruse done. She smiled and teleported back to her hotel room.

Deema

Deema stood outside Kasdeya's apartment door and willed her emotions to settle. The demon would detect any element of fear, despite Queen Linette's charm. Taking a deep breath, she opened the door and entered.

"No dramatic sparks?" Kasdeya twisted to face her from the window. "Where have you been? My spies said you were taken."

"I was." She tilted her head to show the bruise on her cheekbone from where she'd hit the floor after Shayna zapped her. "We were about to leave this world when a shifter attacked. While Shayna was busy fighting, I slipped away."

"Where?" Kasdeya's eyes narrowed.

"Central Park, I think. I was half unconscious." She flopped into the nearest chair.

"Don't worry, my little faerie. I won't let you go anywhere alone again. I thought you could best the blonde. Obviously, I was wrong." She sat across from Deema, her serious gaze not wavering. "One of the human men tried to save you, I hear. Shayna tossed him away like a sack of garbage." Kasdeya smiled.

"Yes." Fear fought to rise. Using all her strength, Deema shoved it down.

"I think we can use him. Befriend the human. Bring him to me. It would work in our favor to have someone spying on sweet, little Shayna."

"Not so sweet." Deema touched the bruise on her face. She couldn't involve the detective. Kasdeya would remove all traces of light and hope from him. Somehow, she'd have to find a way to prevent his coming. "It will be hard to get close to him."

"I trust you'll find a way. If you can't handle the job, I can always assign the task to Radella." Her smile grew colder.

"I'll find a way." Deema stood. At Kasdeya's nod of dismissal, she left via the front door again. Once she'd teleported to the park, her sparks turned a lighter shade of purple, something neither she, Shayna, or the queen had suspected. Already the Light was changing Deema. The demon and Radella would be sure to comment on the lighter color.

Until she could come up with a believable scenario, she'd have to be careful about arriving and leaving.

She hailed a cab and headed to Paddy's pub. He groaned upon seeing her. "Please don't ask me to get involved in anything whatsoever."

She perched on a barstool and slid a piece of paper across the polished counter. "Whiskey, please."

His eyebrows rose, and he pocketed the paper as he poured her a drink. "I thought you didn't like the company of leprechauns."

"I happened to be in the neighborhood." She forced her voice to stay condescending and could only hope the man would deliver her message to Shayna. "It's important that the mail be delivered on time, don't you think? It's going to storm." She surveyed the room to see if anyone paid them undue attention.

"Yeah," he drew the word out, frowning. "But rain doesn't hurt anyone. The post office delivers no matter the weather."

She smiled. He'd gotten the hint. She tossed back the whiskey, suddenly hating the taste, and slid from the stool. She set a ten-dollar bill next to the glass. "Keep the change as a delivery payment." Without another glance his way, she marched from the pub, head held high, a sardonic smile on her face in case anyone watched.

Not seeing anyone following her, she strolled toward her penthouse apartment. When she reached an empty alley, she teleported home in a shower of lavender sparks. Once there, she set a charm to keep followers of both light and dark away and settled down to make a plan to save not only her life, but the lives of Shayna and the detectives.

12

Shayna

"*You tortured her into* submission?" Pierce frowned. "Can we trust her under those circumstances?"

"She wasn't tortured so much as tempted to the point of breaking." Shayna crossed her arms. "Yes, we can trust her now. She passed the test."

Three raps sounded on the door. Shayna held up a finger and placed her other hand on the hilt of the dagger strapped to her thigh. She hadn't taken to wearing her blades outside her armor until things escalated to the point of necessity.

She peered out the peep hole. Not seeing anyone, she yanked the door open, knife at the ready. "Seamus!" A man no more than three feet tall with a head of brilliant white hair grinned up at her.

"Aye, I come bearing a message." He stepped past her, handing her a slip of paper on his way.

"What's to drink?"

"Anything you want." She closed the door and introduced him to the others. "This is Seamus O'Flanagan, leader of the leprechauns, and as ancient as the mountains."

He shook the detectives' hands and climbed onto an empty chair. "Aye, I'm the oldest and the wisest and seven hundred and four." His thick brogue made it difficult to understand him.

Shayna poured the little man a whiskey and read the message. Eyes wide, she said, "Kasdeya wants Payson."

"What?" Payson jerked. "Why me?"

"I don't know. She wants Deema to convince you to join her side."

"Never."

"Hold on." Pierce paced the area in front of the window. "If Deema is a spy for the fae, then why can't you be a spy for the humans?"

"It would be better for you," Seamus said, shooting back his drink. "You being part fae and all. It will be difficult for a mere man to remain true to the Light when surrounded by the dark."

"We need to talk to Deema." Shayna summoned a ball of light no bigger than a firefly and sent it out the window. "She'll come." She turned to Seamus. "Are you actively joining our side? Paddy seemed reluctant."

"The man's a fool, and no lying about it. Coward, too. Yes, we'll fight." Seamus held out his glass. "I love the human's whiskey. Fill'er up, lass."

"Can we get back to the conversation about that demon wanting me?" Payson swallowed hard. "I agree with Seamus. Let Pierce go."

"No." Shayna shook her head. "Radella wants to convert him. He isn't safe without me." It would be hard enough for her to walk away from him when the war was over. If she were to lose him to death…she couldn't bear the thought.

Deema appeared in a shower of sparks. "Cool. Your charm can't keep me out anymore."

Shayna smiled. "It's only against those who follow the dark. Welcome, my friend."

The dark fae glanced at Seamus and grinned. "It's good to see you again. I thought you were dead."

"Not yet." He toasted her with his glass.

"We need more information." Shayna waved the message. "This is a bit cryptic."

"I was in a hurry." She glanced at Payson. "Kasdeya thinks there is darkness in this man because he tried to stop you from taking me."

"She saw us?"

Deema shook her head. "She has spies everywhere, some demons so small they can hide in every corner."

"She believes your story of capture?"

"She does." Deema exhaled heavily. "If this man won't come, I'll have to think of a reason she'll accept."

"This man has a name. It's Clark Payson." Payson's face reddened. "I'm capable of deciding on my own whether I want to take this chance."

"You'd be crazy if you did." Marshal strode to the bathroom and slammed the door.

"He's right." Deema narrowed her eyes. "You'd

be crazy to take the chance."

"If I don't go, what happens to you?"

"It doesn't matter. We're at war. There will be casualties."

Shayna watched the exchange with interest noting a strong connection between the two, similar to what she had with Pierce. "Can you keep him safe?"

"As safe as you keep your human."

The two fae faced off. "His heart is purer than Payson's, and Pierce has leprechaun blood."

Deema glanced at Pierce with new interest. "Really? That's helpful. What can he do?"

Pierce moved a glass from the sideboard, and with one wave of his hand, tossed it at the wall. Shards rained onto the carpet.

"Impressive." Deema's eyes sparkled. "Can you teach him anything else?"

"He isn't a dog to be taught tricks, Deema." Shayna laughed. "It's good to spar with you again—verbally, that is."

Seamus cleared his throat. "I don't think any of us men like being ignored this way." He hopped off his chair. "Call me when you need me." He snapped his fingers and disappeared.

"If he could do that, then why knock?" Marshal said, coming out of the bathroom.

"Dramatics," Shayna said. "Will you train with us?"

"I'd be delighted."

Shayna transported them to the mountaintop. Payson and Marshal didn't throw up this time but still appeared pale. Good. Their bodies were adjusting.

Deema paired immediately with Payson, leaving Shayna to spar with two men at once. Grinning, she held her sword over her head. "Can both of you take me?"

Pierce glanced at Marshal and laughed. "We'd sure like to try." With a warrior yell, he stampeded toward her.

He shot out his leg, tripping her. Good. He improved each time they fought. Before she could get to her feet, Marshal leaned over her. She rolled to her feet. "Time to step up my game and stop taking it easy on you two."

"You've been taking it easy?" Pierce lunged forward, his sword clashing with hers.

She retaliated, then whirled, stopping Marshal from burying his sword in her back. "Well done."

They sparred for an hour before she called a break. "Rest, drink, then I'll teach you some magic."

Pierce

"Finally." Pierce guzzled a bottle of water. He wanted to know exactly what his little bit of fae blood would let him do, although making objects fly through the air was something he could enjoy doing forever.

By the time night started to fall, he'd learned how to start a fire and little else. "I guess I'm not very magical."

"Dude." Marshal clapped him on the back. "If I could make knives fly and hit the target, I'd be satisfied."

"True." He glanced down at the silver-tipped knife in his hand. Shayna had equipped them all with silver daggers and bullets.

"Look." Deema pointed to the other side of the protective dome. "Two shifters."

Pierce flinched at the sight of two enormous wolves watching them. "They're waiting for the shield to lift."

Shayna changed to her armor. So did Deema, whose was as impressive as Shayna's.

"Your cover is blown," Shayna said. "My apologies. I should have made the barrier thicker where no one could see."

"It isn't your fault. How could you predict the shifters knowing where we'd gone? I'm actually relieved. Now, I can openly follow the Light and leave Kasdeya and her followers."

Shayna glanced at Pierce. "You three stay behind us. They're a little different to fight than vampires. Watch and learn."

"Gladly." Pierce and the other two held their swords tight in their hands but took a couple of steps back.

The instant the shield raised, the wolves sprang forward, lunging for the women's throats. The fight that ensued was fast, brutal, and brilliant. Blond hair, dark hair, and the grey of the wolves' fur flew as the four whirled in a fierce battle.

The wolves were quick, but the faeries were

quicker. Yips and war cries filled the air.

Shayna screamed a battlecry that made the hair on Pierce's arms raise, then lifted a wolf and tossed it over her shoulder.

The beast landed at Pierce's feet. Without a second thought, he plunged his sword into its heart. The beast reverted to human form, curled into a fetal position, dead.

The other wolf froze, his yellow stare fixed on Pierce long enough for Shayna to bind it with her silver rope. "Change back to your human form, beast."

With a howl the wolf transformed. A naked man knelt on the ground in front of Shayna.

With a quick glance at the other two detectives, Pierce moved forward. Blood seeped from a bite in Shayna's shoulder. Deema sported claw marks down her arm and thigh. "You're wounded."

"We'll heal." Shayna held her sword at the man's throat. "Why did you follow us?"

"You killed our brother."

"The dragons gave him to me. They killed your brother, not I. I spared him from becoming manure."

The man glared at her. "Small favor."

She pressed the tip to his throat. "This is silver-tipped. Shall I pierce your skin?"

"Do what you wish. I'm alone now."

"Did Kasdeya send you?"

"The demon? No." He shook his head hard enough for his brown curls to fly around his face. "My family does not follow the darkness or the Light. We stay neutral."

"Can we use him?" Pierce asked, moving to Shayna's side.

The man turned to Pierce. "I won't help you."

"Leave us." Shayna whirled around and strode away, motioning for the others to follow her.

"You're letting him go?" Pierce took her arm and turned her to face him. "Won't he tell Kasdeya?"

"Maybe, but we have no reason to hold him."

"He tried to kill you."

"He was mistaken. I cannot kill someone not filled with darkness, unless in self-defense."

Pierce ran his hands through his hair. One moment she was a warrior in battle mode ready to kill, the next she showed compassion. He loved mankind but didn't think he could be as forgiving if someone had attacked him as ferociously as the shifters had the two faeries.

"You don't agree with me."

"You're the boss."

"Yes." She smiled even though a shadow of sadness crossed her face. "It's a role I take seriously, but also one I would like to pass on to another. It is a burden and a great responsibility."

"Why you?"

"Because she is our greatest warrior," Deema said. "Let's return, shall we?"

They transported back to the hotel room where Deema ordered pizza, saying it was her favorite human food. The others flopped on whatever chair they found available.

"We need to go to work," Marshal said, "but every muscle in my body aches."

"Let Shayna touch you. She is a healer." Deema hung up the phone. "I will be again soon, but it takes time for all my powers of the Light to return."

Shayna placed a hand on Marshal's shoulder. Her hand glowed white. "Better?"

"Yes."

She moved on to Payson, then Pierce, letting her touch linger on his shoulder. He put his hand over hers. "You're sad."

She sighed. "Just thinking about the end."

"The end of the war or the end of us," he whispered.

"There is no us." She pulled away.

"There could be, and you know it. You can't use the same excuse you've used in the past about us being too different." He wasn't completely human, thus her reasons for them not having a relationship no longer applied.

The other three watched with interest as Shayna disappeared into the bathroom.

"You could have her bond with you." Deema glanced at the bed. "To our people, that act cements a man and woman together for as long as they live."

As tempting as it was, he wouldn't coerce Shayna into anything she didn't want. "She's the boss. She'll have to initiate the next move."

"She's only the boss as it pertains to the fight." Deema jumped on the bed and spread out on her back. "You're a fool to let her go when this is over. Wake me when the pizza arrives." She closed her eyes.

"These faeries are strange creatures," Payson said, grinning. "I like the sass of this one."

"We need to find me one." Marshal propped his feet on the coffee table. "I'm feeling left out."

"You really want to get involved with a woman of a different kind, from another world? One you can't have?" Payson quirked his mouth. "Look at the turmoil Cochran is going through, and he's one of them."

"Sometimes I wish it would have been someone else deemed worthy enough to have a part in saving the human race." Pierce rested his head against the back of the chair. "You know we probably won't survive this in the end, right?"

"There is that little faith again." Shayna joined them, her hair wet from the shower. "Believe, Pierce. All is not finished until you take your last breath."

He stared into her amazing eyes. "I'll take my last if it means you keep breathing."

13

Shayna

Shayna had seen the truth in Pierce's eyes the night before when he said he'd rather die than lose her. She hadn't slept well because of it. Now, she lay on her side and watched him sleep. Yes, he had fae blood, something for which she was grateful. His added strength would come in handy during battles. But could she allow herself to love him?

A lock of hair had fallen over his forehead. She smoothed it away, careful not to touch him lest he wake. A warrior didn't bond with anyone in her world. Their lives did not lend themselves to romance because of the risk of leaving behind loved ones. She sighed and rolled over to her back.

She did love him. Now what? If only she had someone to advise her. She studied him. His eyes were open. His lips spread in a sexy smile.

"I love sleeping next to you," he said. "I intend

to enjoy it for as long as I can." He propped himself on one elbow. "Where are the others?"

"Deema has appointed herself Payson's guardian. They've gone to her place. Marshal elected to go home."

His eyes widened. "Isn't he in danger, too?"

"I haven't felt so." She flung aside the cotton sheet she'd covered with. "Once I do, we'll make arrangements."

"What's on the agenda today?"

"A normal work day for you until I can find another secure location for us to train." She stood and wrapped her robe around herself.

"It would make things easier for me if you wore a nightgown."

She glanced over her shoulder. "Why? We don't wear them in my world. One's body is nothing to be ashamed of."

"Oh, I'm not ashamed, sweetheart." He grinned and rolled over to his back. "But I am tortured."

"Oh." Her face heated. Tonight, she'd cover herself as the humans did when they slept. How could she have been so insensitive, especially after knowing how Pierce felt about her?

An hour later, in response to a call from the chief demanding they come see him, Shayna marched down the hall of the precinct, the three detectives behind her, and Deema bringing up the rear. Heads turned as they headed for the chief's office.

"Stay here," she told the others. "Pierce, you come with me. The chief isn't alone." She pushed open the door.

Radella gave a cold smile from where she sat across from the chief. "Oh, you're in trouble now," she sang.

"Where have you been, Cochran?" The chief planted his hands flat on his desk and pushed to his feet. "You haven't been reinstated as detective for long and here you go, rough-handling civilians again. This time a woman! And you, Special Agent Sky, are even worse."

"Sir?" Shayna glanced at Pierce.

"Look at her." He pointed to Radella.

Shayna glanced at the still-smiling vampire. "Yes?"

"You've beaten her." He pulled a handkerchief from his pocket and mopped his brow. "A once beautiful face is scarred for life."

"I don't see it, sir." Pierce stood at attention.

Shayna glanced under the desk, narrowing her eyes at the tiny demon sitting there. "Be gone or I'll strike you down."

"Special Agent!" The chief's face darkened. "I'll be filing a complaint against your brutality."

Shayna sighed and touched his shoulder. "It will be all right."

Radella rolled her eyes. "You can't win without your magic, faerie. I'll win with strength and power." She stood, dark eyes dead in a flawless face. "You'll be kept so busy you won't be able to stop the war when it comes. Turning Deema back to the Light will not help you." She swirled to leave, trailing her hand across Pierce's cheek. "Such a waste of good man flesh."

"What in this crazy, upside-down world is going

on here?" The chief glared. "Who was that woman?"

"A nuisance, sir, nothing more. Where would you like us to focus our attentions today?" Shayna smiled.

"Gang activity has increased. See what you can find out." He turned to his computer, dismissing them.

"It's amazing how one touch from you can change the way someone thinks." Pierce chuckled.

"He's easily influenced by the dark." She cast a last glance to where the chief sat. "That doesn't bode well for this city if all the leaders can be so easily manipulated."

"I could hardly restrain myself from ridding us all of her presence." Deema snarled.

"Why didn't you?" Shayna studied her angry face.

"She threatened to destroy the place and everyone inside this building." She crossed her arms. "You're going to have to trust me if we're going to make this work."

Her friend was right, but so was Radella. Stress weighed on shoulders that had never felt the burden before. Two faeries and three human law officers could not be everywhere they needed to be. She mentally grumbled against her queen's order to do everything she could to prevent an all-out war. It was too much for one warrior to handle.

"You aren't alone." Pierce took her hand.

"You're reading my mind now?" She forced a smile.

"No, your thoughts are on your face and in the

slump of your shoulders." He motioned toward the other three. "We're in this together. You said help would come when it was needed."

"That's right. We can handle the minor skirmishes." She squeezed his hand. "Thank you."

"I'm glad I could comfort you for once. You always seem to be the one who heals."

Radella

Radella hated traitors more than anything else. It had taken all her will power not to extinguish Deema's life. The dark-haired faerie's time would come, and Radella would make sure she was the one responsible.

She stormed to where Dan waited. "How many did you convert?"

"Two." He picked at his fingernails with the tip of a pocketknife.

"That's all?" She slapped him.

"I took my time with them." He glowered and stepped back. "An immortal man has to take his fun where he can get it."

"Not at the expense of our side not winning the coming war. We need fighters." She gave him a two-handed shove, slamming him back against the solid brick wall. "Do not disobey my orders again or you won't have to worry about being immortal. I'll turn you to ash myself." She stomped from the alley and hailed a taxi, leaving the imbecile to find his own way.

She gave the driver Kasdeya's address and formulated in her mind the reason she hadn't killed Deema. Nothing she came up with was a reason the demon would accept. Still, she hadn't fled like the imp under the desk. That idiot was history.

At the high-rise complex Kasdeya resided in, Radella knocked and waited for the order to enter. When she received it, she stepped inside.

Kasdeya stared out the window. "Tell me what happened."

If she'd been human, Radella would have taken a deep breath before continuing. "I had the chief-of-police convinced I'd been beaten by Cochran and Shayna, but then she touched him. May I cut off her hands?" She forced a laugh.

"Perhaps, I'll cut off yours." She pivoted to face her. "I gather she found the one I sent to influence the man?"

"With two words from her lips, he fled."

Kasdeya studied her so long she started to fidget. "I'll summon him. You will stay and see what I do to those who don't follow my orders."

"I couldn't take out Deema at the station. Not with Shayna and the part—"

"Yes, I know the one detective is part fae. It makes no difference. He doesn't have enough power to matter. Shayna is another story. Somehow we've got to make her lose her faith in the Light."

The imp who failed at his job appeared and bowed. Not impressive considering he couldn't be more than six inches tall.

"Observe, Radella, and remember." Kasdeya

grinned and picked him up with two fingers. She tore him appendage from appendage, limb from limb. The demon's agonizing screams reverberated to the point Radella covered her ears, then Kasdeya stomped him into nothing more than charred paper. With a soft blow, she made him vanish in a puff of smoke. She rubbed her hands together. "Now I trust you got the point?"

Pierce

It felt good to return to something akin to routine even if the two groups of teenage boys were fighting because of the swarm of demons flying around their heads. Pierce flashed the lights on top of the car and laughed as half the boys scattered. "Let's take care of the ones itching to fight a police officer." He shoved his door open.

"Do not hurt them," Shayna said. "They aren't in control."

"I'm not going to hurt them." Maybe rough them up a little. "You think nothing of killing someone from the dark side but balk at injuring humans. Not all of those boys you see have a glimmer of light left in them. A couple of them were born dark, I guarantee it."

"There is no such thing. All living creatures contain both good and the ability to do evil. It's the side you choose. These young men need the opportunity to choose the right side." Shayna strolled toward them despite bawdy comments and gestures.

Her customary white glow started, and the comments stopped. Within five minutes, three young men sat in the back of the squad car and two were sent home. "You're partially right," she told Pierce as she slid into the front seat. "These boys in the back just need a little more convincing than the others."

"Like what?"

"Some time in a holding cell with me." She grinned.

He laughed and started the car. "I can't wait to see this."

He didn't get a chance. While Shayna led the boys to be booked, Pierce got called into the chief's office. He held up a hand to quiet the chief and searched for a demon. Not finding one, he took his position across the desk. "Sir?"

"I'm not even going to ask what all that was about." The chief ruffled through some papers. "I'm retiring in three months. I'm on the lookout for a new chief." He peered up from under bushy brows. "I'm considering you."

Pierce wished Shayna was nearby to tell him whether the chief had been influenced or not. "Are you unwell?"

"Cancer. It's okay. I'm resigned to the fact. Stage four prostate." He leaned back in his chair. "What do you think?"

What he honestly thought was that Shayna needed to put her hand on the man's private parts and heal him but doubted that would go over well with her or the chief. "This city is losing a good man, sir. I'm sorry to hear it. Have you tried radiation or chemo?"

"I've elected not to." He leaned his elbows on the table. "I've lived a good life, but I'm alone. No wife, no kids, no one to miss me. If it's my time, it's my time."

"I'm honored to be considered as your replacement, but I'm not sure I'll still be in New York."

"Why not?"

"I've a nicer place in mind, sir." One full of gold and crystal and Shayna in a gauzy dress. "You're still alive and kicking, sir. Don't give up hope now."

"Since when did you become such a Pollyanna?"

"Since meeting Shayna, sir. You should spend some time in her company. It's good for what ails you." He grinned and backed from the room, then headed for the holding cell.

No sign of Shayna, but the boys looked contrite and slightly shell-shocked. Good. Maybe they'd turn away from their old ways after all.

14

Shayna

"*I can't do it* alone." Shayna bowed before her queen. "My faith is faltering. The darkness grows faster than I can stop it."

"You aren't alone, my dear." Queen Linette placed a hand on her shoulder. "Come with me. I've something to show you." She glanced at Pierce who waited at the back of the room. "You, too, detective. You're one of us, after all."

White gown fluttering behind her like angel wings, the queen led them outside and through trees dripping with moss until they entered a clearing. A group of faeries, light and dark-haired, sparred with swords.

In answer to Shayna's unspoken question, Queen Linette answered, "With Deema's return to the Light, several of the dark-hairs have joined us. My hope is that someday we'll all fight together against evil. I have a couple that can join you now, but I fear that would be a show of force and start the war before we are fully prepared."

Pierce took Shayna's hand in his. "I'll stand by her. I won't let Shayna falter from doing what needs done."

"I have complete faith that you will be there." The queen smiled. "A moment of privacy with Shayna, please."

He nodded and moved closer to the training warriors.

"He loves you," Queen Linette said.

"This is not the time for such things. A warrior should not love, bond, and have a family."

"Why not?" Queen Linette tilted her head. "Are warriors so special they must live their lives alone? That's a long time in our world."

"My mother died fighting the darkness and left *me* alone." Shayna raised her gaze to meet her queen's. "I won't do that to someone I care about."

Queen Linette cupped her cheek. "Foolish girl. Love reigns over all. Don't deprive yourself of something beautiful." She glanced to where Pierce stood. "He's a good man."

"I don't want to leave The Glen."

"Then don't. Love will work it out. Perhaps he will want to live here. You spurned Earin's proposal decades ago. This could be the man for you."

She glanced at Pierce. "I'll think about it." Shayna bowed, then moved to Pierce's side. She studied his strong jaw and the interest in his eyes. Could the queen be right? Could love be worth any price?

Pierce smiled down at her. "Let's spar with

them."

She grinned. "Absolutely. It'll be fun." She pulled her sword from her scabbard and advanced.

The fighters stopped and bowed as she moved through them.

"At ease, warriors. I'm one of you. Do not think you need to take it easy on either one of us."

A white-haired faerie with dark eyes smirked, his gaze hard. "Not even on the human?"

"Not even on him." Shayna tossed Pierce a grin. "He can handle himself, Earin." She tapped her sword on the faerie's shoulder. "Commence."

The clanging of swords rang again over the clearing. After an hour, hope swelled again in Shayna's breast. These were worthy fighters. For the first time in days, she believed they could win against the darkness.

After the training session and the others had gone, she reclined in a patch of fragrant clover with Pierce. "You've become good," she said, staring into his eyes. "Your attitude has softened since I met you, your language no longer crude."

He chuckled. "Hanging around you is good for me."

"Hmm." She lay on her back and stared at the clouds floating in front of the three suns. She'd needed this day in The Glen. A day of rejuvenation and a conversation with her queen. Tomorrow would be another day fighting the darkness. She'd take rest where she could find it. Her traitorous heart leaped at the thought of spending the day with Pierce.

Pierce reached over and entwined a strand of her

hair around his finger. "I never thought anyone as beautiful as you existed."

She faced him. "All the faeries are beautiful," she whispered, although she did love hearing him say the words.

"Not as beautiful as you." He leaned over and kissed her.

This time she didn't pull back but rather enjoyed the feel of his lips on hers and deepened the kiss. Here, she couldn't read his thoughts; here she was an ordinary woman enjoying the attentions of a handsome, kind man who held her heart.

He moved closer. "Am I being inappropriate?" he whispered against her lips.

"Yes." She smiled. "But do continue." They were alone, but not too private to where things could spiral to a point there was no turning back. Without more searching of her heart, she couldn't make the commitment Pierce desired. Not yet.

Pierce

Pierce couldn't remember a better day than the one he had just spent with Shayna. Now back in her hotel room, he waited for the others to join them. Shayna would inform them the faeries were preparing for battle. At the moment, she stood in front of the large window, cup of coffee in hand, gazing at the sky.

"They seem agitated," she said.

Pierce joined her. The dark shapes dipped and swirled, rose and fell, with no obvious purpose in mind. The two vampires keeping guard on the sidewalk in front of the hotel paced nervously, casting glances up and down the street.

"What do you think is happening?"

She shrugged. "No idea, but they're upset about something."

"Could it have to do with seeing Radella at the station yesterday?"

"That or they've heard of our growing forces." She took a sip of her drink. "I'm hoping it's the latter. If so, they aren't as strong as they want us to believe."

Deema, Payson, and Marshal entered, locking the door behind them. "Something's shaking." Deema grinned and plopped on the bed.

Pierce turned. "Any idea what?"

"Nope. Was hoping you two lollygaggers could tell us." She crossed her arms behind her head. "While the two of you relaxed in The Glen, we three were working and took out two more vamps." Her smile faded. "Radella is stepping up her game in converting humans. There're more every day."

"We did more than take the day off," Shayna said, transferring her attention to Deema. "We trained with dark-haired faeries."

Deema sat up. "What? They've joined us?"

"Quite a few have. I have hope that more will before the great war begins."

Payson frowned. "Are the light and dark haired divided?"

Deema nodded. "Have been for centuries.

Hundreds of years ago, there were two sisters, or so the story goes. One fair of hair, the other dark." She flipped her ebony hair over her shoulder clearly pleased at telling a story.

Pierce and the others sat to listen. Pierce enjoyed a good story, same as any other man. He patted his leg, inviting Shayna to sit in his lap.

Her cheeks darkened, and she chose a chair next to him. "We aren't alone."

"Who cares?" He winked.

Deema cleared her throat to get their attention. "As I was saying, there were two sisters, both vying for the attention of the prince. The prince was the most handsome creation ever made, but he had a seed of arrogance in his heart. He liked the attention of both sisters and refused to choose between them. In his lust and greed, he wanted them both. They refused. Then," she paused dramatically, "he proposed a duel to the death. At that time they both saw through his handsomeness and refused him again. He banished them to different corners of our world."

"What happened to the prince?" Pierce asked. "Are there three groups of faeries?"

She shook her head. "He married another and died at the old age of a nine hundred and one. Those who followed him chose sides. Light and dark hair once lived together in harmony."

"Even in our world, problems exist," Shayna said. "Not like they do in your world, but we do have our challenges."

Marshal rubbed his hands together. "The good news is not only are the dark side numbers growing, but our side is, too. I'm starting to enjoy kicking vampire as...butt." He glanced sheepishly at Shayna.

"Now what?" Payson asked. "We wait?"

"No." Pierce leaned forward. "We keep doing what we're doing until we stop Radella."

"How?" he asked.

"With Shayna's silver rope."

All heads turned in her direction. Shayna thought for a moment. "What's your plan? Mine was to kill her and rid the world of her evil."

"I was thinking capture. Maybe we can use her as a bargaining tool to get the other vampires to step down." Pierce crossed his arms. "It sometimes works in interrogations. If nothing else, maybe we can force her to divulge Kasdeya's weaknesses."

"She doesn't have any," Deema said.

"Everyone has a weakness. Yours is iron."

Deema narrowed her eyes at Shayna. "You let them know our weakness? Did you also tell them how to kill us?"

"Of course not, but the iron came into play once, and I had to tell."

Pierce stiffened. "I think we should know what kills you. Otherwise, how can we prevent it from happening?" He'd step in front of a bullet for Shayna, or a fireball, whatever it was that could kill her.

Deema and Shayna clashed gazes, clearly speaking silently as to how much information to divulge. Deema must not have liked Shayna's decision because she stormed to the bathroom.

"We will promise not to use it against you."

Pierce held out his hand. "Guys?"

They held hands with Shayna. Electricity flowed through Pierce and into Payson. "What are you doing?"

"Binding your tongue. It's the only way you can't tell anyone, even under torture." Shayna sighed. "It may sound silly to you, but lemon juice will kill us."

"Not a stab to the heart?" Marshal narrowed his eyes.

"Well, that will, also, but that kills anyone. Each race has their weakness. The vampires and shifters are allergic to silver. Us…simple human lemon juice is the same as acid to us."

Kasdeya

Something was going on in the faerie world. Something that did not bode well for Kasdeya and her minions. Curse Radella for not ridding them of Deema when she had the chance. She snarled. After yesterday's demonstration, the vampire would think twice about disobeying an order.

Doing something she rarely did, Kasdeya left her apartment. As she strode down the sidewalk, humans and demons alike moved out of her way. She laughed. The humans had no idea why she intimidated them, only that she did. Simple-minded fools.

She stopped in front of Shayna's hotel. Kasdeya

couldn't penetrate the barrier, but she could let them know she knew their location. Leaning against a light post across the street, she crossed her arms and ankles and waited for someone to look out the window.

Ah, one of the detectives. The dark-haired one with hazel eyes. Marshal, she remembered Deema, the traitor, telling her about the officer. She smiled up at him.

He continued to meet her gaze, unintimidated by her presence. Fury rose inside her. She made a fire ball between her hands and threw it at the window. It hit the glass and rained hot embers on the passing pedestrians.

Shayna immediately appeared in a shower of ice blue sparks.

"I really hate how fancy you faeries are." Kasdeya pretended to study her nails. "Why can't you just flutter your little wings to get around? Could it be they're too weak to hold you?"

"Why are you here?" Shayna glared, her ridiculous blue gaze not wavering.

"Boredom. I thought things might be more interesting at your place, but it's more boring than I imagined." She pushed away from the pole. "Have you realized the futility of fighting me yet? Join me, pretty little faerie, and have more power than you ever imagined."

"I'm fine where I am, thank you."

Kasdeya scowled. "Don't you ever get tired of the goody-goody act? I know there is still division among your people. It wouldn't take much for your world to fall." Stupid people of the Light. Oh, how she wanted to extinguish the Light they followed.

"You can try."

"I'll do more than try, pretty girl." Kasdeya reached out to pat Shayna's cheek, only to find her hand thrust brutally away. She laughed. "You do have anger in you. That is good news. Anger is a seed that I can nurture. Until next time, my dear." She pivoted and strolled away, the skin on the back of her neck prickling as if the faeries' gaze were swords digging into her back.

Why hadn't Shayna attacked? What game were the fae of the Light playing? Gaining control of Kasdeya would halt the evil from spreading. Stupid faeries. She would not be so lenient on them should the opportunity present itself.

15

Shayna

The air outside crackled with electricity, drifting through the open window of the car. Every one of Shayna's senses were on alert. She glanced at Pierce in the driver's seat. "Call the others. Something big is happening."

"We haven't received a call from the precinct."

"You will."

He contacted his partners and Deema. "Be ready. Shayna said—"

The radio in his dash spouted an alert. "Hostage situation on Broadway. Lou's Grocery. No idea how many are inside. All units respond."

"Detective Cochran and Special Agent Sky on it." Pierce responded and turned on the siren.

Soon, they halted next to several squad cars parked behind wooden barricades in front of a small mom-and-pop food store. Shayna shoved open her door and headed to the barrier, focusing all her attention on the store.

Steel grates, usually only used after-hours to protect the store from break-ins, covered the one large window in front. Someone had tacked butcher paper over the front glass door to keep people from looking inside. "Who's in charge here?" She stared at the officers taking cover behind open car doors.

"You are now," Officer Charges said, "and we're glad of it."

"Any demands made?"

He shook his head. "We've tried calling, but no one answers the phone. The only other access, a steel back door, is bolted shut. No access from the roof."

Shayna focused her attention on the store as Marshal, Payson, and Deema arrived on the scene. Deema joined her. "I sense three influenced people and ten innocents," Shayna said. "I'm trying to find a way to get inside without harming them."

"Fire ball to the front door. Blast it open."

She cut Deema a sharp gaze. "An idea like that is why I'm in charge."

Deema shrugged. "I doubt anyone is leaning against the door. Force it open, get inside, and take out the bad guys."

"Hmm." Shayna climbed over the barrier and approached the store.

"Wait!" Pierce started to follow her.

"No one comes along except for Deema." Her voice left no room for argument.

Pierce's face darkened, but he remained on the other side, stepping away as Deema went to join Shayna. "We'll be discussing this later," he said.

She had no doubt. She stopped a few feet from the door and waited to see whether someone would acknowledge her presence. When no one did, she glanced at Deema. "Could they all be dead and magic put in place so we don't know?"

"Would have to be some powerful magic. Our people are the strongest. None of the other races come close." Deema cupped her hands around her eyes and peered through a small space between the paper and the door frame. "Three hostiles wearing black and a bunch of frightened humans sitting on the floor by the cash registers."

"Why aren't they trying to contact us?" Her eyes widened at the sight of Earin climbing over the barrier. This would not be good news.

"Alvar has joined Kasdeya." Sadness clouded his features.

Shock ricocheted through her. "He's our strongest user of magic." She glanced at the store. "He's behind this?"

"Queen Linette believes so."

Powerful magic. Something would be in place to trigger an action if a wrong move was made. Shayna took Deema's place peering in the window. *There he is*. A tall silver-haired faerie sat perched on the corner of the deli counter. The humorless smirk on his face told her he knew she stood outside and watched.

He said something to one of the armed men and the man opened his jacket to reveal a bomb. He then pulled the trigger on his AR-15 and sprayed the ceiling with bullets. The hostages cowered and screamed as plaster and glass fell on them.

"He's going to blow the place up." Shayna's blood chilled. "I don't know how to stop him. Please tell me the Queen has an idea."

Earin shrugged. "She said to do whatever is necessary to stop him. His magic is too strong to allow him to live if he chose the dark."

"But I don't know what to do." Tears stung the back of her throat. If she could fight Alvar with a sword, things would be in her favor. She was a strong fighter with magic, but no match for the elder faerie inside.

She made her way through the confused police officers to where Pierce and the other two detectives waited. "We have a problem."

"We figured as much when he showed up," Pierce said, motioning his head to Earin. "What's happening?"

She quickly explained the situation, heart-broken at the fallen features of those listening. "We've got to clear the street. Now." She barked orders to the uniformed officers, sending them scurrying up and down the street knocking on doors. At the least they could minimize casualties.

She turned as Chief Rosen arrived, his belly jiggling under his white shirt as he rushed toward them. "Fill me in."

When she finished, he grabbed a bullhorn from the nearest squad car. "Inside the building. Pick up the phone!" He snapped his fingers. "Somebody dial the number to that store."

Payson did and handed the chief his cell phone. "Sir, the negotiator hasn't arrived."

"I'll negotiate." He called the store, listened,

then handed the phone to Shayna. "They'll only speak to you."

"Yes, Alvar?" Shayna held the phone to her ear while keeping her eyes on the store. "Why bother calling, or have you put a shield of protection in place that keeps me from mentally communicating with you?"

"Aren't you the clever little girl?" His smooth voice rolled through the airwaves.

"Why are you doing this?"

"Because the one I now follow commanded it. Aren't we faeries good at taking orders?"

Shayna bit her lower lip. "What do you want?"

"You and Deema to come inside. Leave Earin out there. He's no worry to us…yet."

"That's it?"

"That's it." He laughed. "Let me know when you're ready." He hung up.

She handed the phone back to Payson. "He wants Deema and I to go inside."

"Absolutely not," Pierce and the chief said in unison.

"I'll not lose a single law enforcement officer over this." He turned to the arriving SWAT van. "Get me a sniper!"

Payson's phone rang. After listening to the voice on the other end, he handed it to Shayna. "You might as well keep it."

"Dear Shayna, do tell that large man to stop shrieking. It grates on my nerves." Alvar's laugh sent chills down her spine. "He's only making the humans with the guns nervous. A sniper is not effective against the shield I've put up."

"I'll come in now. Let the people go."

"Not yet, dear." Click.

"We do nothing but wait," she told the others. "A sniper is ineffective."

"What nonsense are you spouting?" Chief Rosen stormed to the SWAT team. "Get me someone in place on the building behind us. Take the shot when you can."

Shayna flicked the demon off his shoulder.

He whirled. "What are you doing?"

"A pest, sir." She smiled, reaching to rest her hand on him.

"Step back. You're out of line." Tossing one last glare her way, he stormed back to the barricade.

"I don't see any more demons on him," Pierce said. "But, this is definitely not the way he normally acts. Can they be invisible to you?"

She shook her head, studying the man who leaned against the van. "There is one, but it must be hiding in his clothing. I can't do anything short of tackling him." She glanced at the rooftops, finally spotting Radella and Kasdeya on top of a drugstore. They were there to watch the explosion.

Dread filled Shayna. There was nothing she could do to prevent what was going to happen, and they were using the chief to help things move quickly toward devastation. "The moment Deema and I enter that store, it will blow."

"If we both cast a shield over us, a double shield," Deema said, "we can protect ourselves."

"But not those inside."

"No."

The phone in her hand rang. "Yes."

"It's time, dear. Come on in. The sniper is putting his finger on the trigger as we speak."

She glanced at the store door. The paper had been pulled down, and Alvar wiggled his fingers at her. "Come in, and I will spare all but the shooters."

"You lie."

"You know I am incapable of lying, same as you."

"The more darkness, the easier it is to tell untruths."

"Will you take the chance?"

"Yes." This time she hung up.

"Don't do it. Please." Pierce wrapped his arms around her. "Or at least let me come along."

"I can't. I'll be all right. You would surely die if you came." She gazed into his eyes, not telling him that the chance of her returning was slim. "I'll be back."

"Promise?"

She placed a tender kiss on his lips, then cupped his cheek. "Stay behind the SWAT van. I can't be worrying about you." She took a deep breath, and with Deema at her side, approached the building.

"He'll be expecting something from us," Deema said.

"He won't know we've placed a shield. Alvar will think we came because of our love for humans." Shayna placed her shield around them as Deema did the same. No man-made explosion could harm them unless Alvar had cast a spell to make their shield ineffective. She prayed he hadn't created a bomb from magic.

The door swung open as they approached.

A shot rang out.

The chief raced toward them. "Not yet."

The armed man closest to them pressed the detonator, and the world filled with fire.

Heat rolled over the shield in waves. Shayna watched in horror as those in the store were blown to bits and the building fell around her and Deema. She whirled to glance behind them.

The chief lay in the street. He'd managed to come halfway before the shot was fired. Alvar was nowhere to be seen.

Alvar's laugh rang in her ears. "Your shield is melting, my lovelies. Do take your time getting out."

Shayna grabbed Deema's hand as the fire burned their shield. They darted back outside. Her skin burned, her jacket singed around the edges. She'd tend to her wounds later. She scanned the area for any sign of the evil faerie and the demon he followed. There. Racing across the roof.

She transported and landed in front of them. "Let's end this."

"Not yet." Kasdeya grinned. "There's a lot more fun coming in the future." Radella grabbed her hand and snapped her fingers, teleporting them away.

16

Shayna

Shayna fell to her knees. "No."

She'd lost them again and human lives in the process. Queen Linette was wrong to put her in charge. The task was too great. Shards of pain ripped through her heart.

Deema appeared by her side and knelt next to her. "You're needed below. There are injuries."

She glanced into a face marked by flying glass. Deema's clothes were as badly singed as Shayna's. "Pierce?"

"A few cuts. Come." She stood and held out her hand. "It's the chief you need to see first. I can heal the minor wounds, but my strength isn't as strong as yours yet."

Every part of her body screamed as she rose to her feet. It took great effort for her to transport to the street below. Her legs threatened to buckle as she landed. She'd be fine after a while, but the explosion had wreaked havoc, and the magic it contained would make it take longer for her to heal. Even longer if she used her powers to heal the mortally wounded, something she would risk.

Casting a quick glance at Pierce who sat in the back of the ambulance getting his cuts tended to, she knelt next to the chief. Blood seeped from where a large piece of glass had imbedded in his chest. "Sir?"

"Special Agent." He coughed, spraying her face with his blood. "No idea why I ran into the street, only that I had the irresistible urge to follow you."

"It was a foolish move." She studied the shard. "I can heal you, sir."

"No need. I'm dying anyway. Prostate cancer."

"I can heal that, too."

His eyes widened, and he coughed again. "Who are you?"

"Shayna of The Glen." She decided to tell him all and worry about the consequences later. "Part of the realm of fae sent here to try and rid your world of darkness. There's an approaching war, sir. The precinct needs you to lead them."

"Don't toy with me. Such things don't exist."

She summoned a ball of light to appear in the palm of her hand. "All I need to do is place this on your injuries. My touch will heal you."

"Magic tricks. Cochran will take my place. I'm ready to die." Tears rolled down his fat cheeks. "Everything happens for a reason, am I right?"

She nodded. Kasdeya wanted the chief out of the way so Pierce would be too busy to help Shayna. It was one more way of chipping away at

Shayna's faith. It worked, too. She lowered her hand. "Please, sir. Pierce is needed elsewhere."

He gripped her hand. "Maybe you are who you say you are. I feel something when I hold your hand, but lady…I've done a lot of bad in my life, treated women poorly, and now it's time to pay the piper. Let me go."

Pierce knelt next to them and put a hand on the chief's shoulder. "Shayna is right. We need you, sir."

The man shook his head and closed his eyes. "You're the chief now." He breathed his last.

Shayna raised her face to the sky and screamed. All her pain, all her frustrations released in the primal sound. Those nearby covered their ears.

"Stop, baby." Pierce took her in his arms. "We can do this."

She shook her head and vanished, reappearing in front of the portal that would lead her home. The medics would care for the humans. Shayna needed healing of another kind. A kind she could only find in her world.

Rather than go to her hut, she summoned Crystal and flew to visit the dragons. As soon as she approached, two sentries flew on either side of her. Not a nice welcome. She could only hope Gorna hadn't changed her mind about helping in the fight.

The large blue dragon waited in the center of the clearing, a hard look in her yellow eyes. "Dismount, Shayna."

She did and kneeled in front of Gorna. "I need your help."

"The time for battle is not now." Her harsh

voice rolled over Shayna. "We've discussed this."

"Is that why you sent an escort?"

"No, danger is escalating. We take no chances."

Shayna looked up. "It's not the war kind of help. I need my strength renewed, and only you can help me. With your scales covering my armor, we are bound warriors." She blinked back tears. "You cannot refuse me, and I've never asked before."

"You've never had a need before. Come, your tears show you are feeling weak." The dragon lowered her neck for Shayna to climb on her back, then with a mighty whoosh of her wings, soared into the air. Minutes later, they landed next to a pool surrounded by gems as big as mountains. Gorna had brought Shayna to the very place she'd hoped. The sacred pool of strengthening.

She slid to the ground. "I thank you. This is my last hope at beating Kasdeya."

"You have hope enough." The dragon's gaze softened. "You are worthy enough, Shayna. Strong enough, although right now you look a little tattered." Her lip curled. "Your queen will be disappointed you didn't come to her with your worries."

"No." Shayna stripped. "She'd be disappointed at my failure." She stepped into the cool waters and submerged.

Immediately her burns cooled, her cuts pain free. Closing her eyes, she floated on the water's surface and breathed deeply, letting the water heal not only her physical pains but her emotions. Faith sprang new in her breast. Strength returned to her limbs. When she'd reached complete relaxation, she emerged from the water and rested on the bank. A crystal vial perched on top of a rock.

"Take some of the water with you," Gorna said. "The vial will never run empty as long as both you and I live. You will need your strength renewed again in the days to come. Caution, Shayna. Do not rely too much on the water. It can be as addictive as the human drugs can be to them. Weaning oneself is difficult."

"I understand, and my gratitude is endless." Shayna dressed and tucked the vial into a pocket of her armor. "I am truly blessed to wear your scales."

"I'm glad they protect you." Gorna lowered her neck again to return them to where Crystal waited. When Shayna dismounted again, the dragon said, "Remember my words. Only use the water when you are at your lowest."

Pierce

"Where have you been?" Pierce stopped pacing in front of the hotel window when Shayna appeared. Anger boiled under his skin. "You scream like a banshee, give me a tortured look, and vanish. I thought you'd die. You could have." He ran his hands through his hair. "I have no idea what happens when a faerie dies. You've been gone for hours."

"I'm sorry. I've been renewing, something I had to do, or I'd be no good to anyone." She sat in a chair. "Where are the others?"

"Resting at Deema's. No one walked away from that explosion unscathed." He crossed his arms, refusing to let her pained look ease his anger. "You could have told me. You went to The Glen?"

"The dragons."

"You don't have a mark on you, so it must have worked. Deema still shows signs of her injuries." He sat across from her and forced his blood pressure to lower. "Are you okay?"

She nodded. "The dragons have powerful healing properties if they choose to let you use them. Since Gorna's scales cover my armor, she can't refuse me unless we fight for opposite sides." Her eyes shimmered as her gaze met his. "I had nothing left in me to fight with. I had to go. We lost thirteen innocent people today, counting the chief. My heart was shattered. It's bad enough to lose one innocent, but several at a time is too much for me."

He moved to her side on the bed and, cupping her face, wiped away her tears. "It happens in war, sweetheart." He pulled her head to his chest. "When you screamed, I thought I'd lost you, you were so shattered. I promised your queen to lift you up when you needed it. Why won't you let me?"

"You would have died today if you'd been with me. Our shields would not have covered you enough during the blast."

"But you rarely let me even try." He tilted her face to his. "I want to try."

"Don't you see?" She shook her head. "This was all planned to the last detail. The explosion, the chief's death. Alvar knew the chief was influenced, knew he'd come to take charge. He wanted Chief Rosen to die so you could take his place."

"So?"

"That means you'll be too busy to be there for me. You have much more responsibility now. Because of that, I had to find something else to keep me strong." She pulled a vial from her pocket.

"What is that?"

"Sacred water. It will keep me strong."

"Sounds like a magical drug." He reached for it. "You don't need it. You're strong enough."

She held it away from him. "Do not presume to know what is best for me." She pocketed the water and stood. "We must rest. Tomorrow will be another tough day. Kasdeya will keep up her games until we're too exhausted to be of any use in the fight."

He clamped his jaw tight and undressed. Climbing into bed, he pulled up the sheet and turned his back to Shayna. He didn't care about his role as the new chief. It was far more important to him to keep her safe and uplifted. He'd delegate as many duties as he could and make sure he remained by Shayna's side.

If Alvar was a faerie, then Pierce knew just what would take care of the evil fae. He just needed to get close enough.

17

Shayna

Shayna changed from the cotton nightgown she slept in to her everyday clothes. Mornings started much quicker when one didn't worry about what to wear as the humans did.

She glanced to where Pierce tightened his tie, relieved to see the worry lines from the day before vacant from his face. He caught her reflection in the mirror and smiled. Her breath caught at the tenderness in his gaze. Today was his first day behind a desk, and her first day in a long time without him by her side. She already missed him and almost reached for the vial in her pocket. No, Gorna had been explicit about the dangers of over-imbibing.

"You make a very handsome chief-of-police." It took a lot of effort to keep her smile from trembling.

"Thanks." He turned from the mirror. "Let's

head to the precinct, say hello, and hit the streets looking for Kasdeya and her newest toy."

It all sounded good, but from the moment they entered the precinct, Pierce became embroiled in the day-to-day running of things, leaving Shayna waiting on the outskirts. The former receptionist quit, to be replaced with one with tight clothes, bright red lipstick, and blond hair too high to be normal without a large amount of back-combing. While Pierce explained what the woman's duties were, she focused on filing her nails until Shayna had enough and approached the counter.

Snatching the file from the woman's hand, she said, "Listen when your new chief is speaking or find another job."

"Way to make my first day drama-free," Pierce said, shooting her a frustrated look. "But Agent Sky is right. Either be professional or walk out the front door. That goes for all of you." He surveyed the others in the room. "It is not my choice to be here. Chief Rosen chose me. We all have to make the best of it and get the job done. Now," he held out his hand to the receptionist, Amber. "Messages."

She rolled her eyes. "Forwarded to your email. This ain't my first rodeo."

"Then act like it isn't." With a nod to Shayna, he marched to his office. Inside, he closed the door and sat behind the desk. "It won't last. Everyone just needs to get used to me."

Shayna sat across from him. "They are used to you. You've been a detective here for a long time." And so it began. The daily tasks of running a big city police department would consume Pierce's time until Kasdeya set up his death the same way she had Chief Rosen. The difference? Pierce's heart was in the right place, where the other man was easily influenced. "I'll be okay with Deema and the others. Is there anything we need to handle or should I begin my hunt?"

"You're going to start hunting Kasdeya?" His eyes widened. "What happened to waiting and letting her make a move?"

"That didn't work so well yesterday, did it?" She sighed. "I'm going on the…offensive, as you say. I can make things as difficult for her as she does for me."

"Do you have a plan?" He leaned back in his chair.

"Not yet, but Deema and I will come up with one."

He motioned his head toward the door. "Speaking of."

Smiling, Shayna turned.

Deema glared through the small window in the door before opening it an inch, signs of the explosion still on her face. "Pierce, the roof of this entire precinct is swarming with demons."

"I'll take care of it." He groaned.

"It's best to wait until I can." Shayna stood and opened the door. "Come with me, Deema. Please." She led her to the bathroom and tore off a piece of toilet tissue. "I have something to heal your cuts." She poured a bit of the water on the tissue and dabbed at Deema's wounds.

"What is that?" Deema sniffed. "It smells like flowers."

"Really?" Shayna took a sniff. "When I floated in the pool, I thought it smelled of fresh air and sunshine."

"Maybe it smells like whatever makes us happy." She narrowed her eyes. "Gorna took you to the sacred pool?"

"Yes. I desperately needed it."

Deema frowned. "I haven't spoken to the dragon in decades. I suppose we're no longer connected after my switching sides."

"You could try to reconcile." Shayna stepped back and watched the cuts close. "Here. One sip will renew your strength. One, but no more."

Deema's eyes brightened as she took a sip and handed back the bottle. "Wow. I want some of that."

"You know where to find it." Shayna leaned against the counter. "We need a plan to shake up Kasdeya's world the same way she's shaking up ours. I'd like to come up with one without the interference of Pierce and the others. They don't know her like we do and will say it's too dangerous."

"Agreed. So what?"

"We need to turn someone as they did Alvar." Shayna tried to think of someone and came up empty. "Demons are no good, nor are vampires. We need a flesh-and-blood creature."

"A shifter? Maybe we could find one that chose the wrong side."

"How?" The thought held merit.

"We ask around. Someone will know something."

"I'd rather have someone with great power."

"No one has more magic than the faeries."

"True." Shayna huffed. She jerked. "Wait a minute. It's a long shot, but…we need a wizard."

"They don't exist." Deema shook her head. "They died out long ago."

"I don't think so. I think one still lives as a hermit in the mystical woods outside The Glen. Will you come with me to see?"

"Sure." She shrugged. "I'm always up for a wild goose chase."

Shayna flashed Pierce a smile as they passed his office. He glanced up frowning, clearly annoyed at the officer standing in front of him. He held up a finger for her to wait.

She shook her head and stepped out the back door of the building to reappear in front of the portal.

Pierce

Pierce glanced at the clock on the wall. "Did you just waste fifteen minutes of my time complaining about the quality of the coffee in the break room?"

"It's horrible." Officer Charges shuddered. "Tastes like oil left in a pail for ten years."

"Get out of my sight." Pierce turned back to his computer. Two seconds didn't go by before Marshal barged into his office.

"What makes you the choice for chief?" His face darkened. "I've got seniority."

"No idea. Wasn't my choice." Pierce focused his attention on his partner. "We'll have to wait and see what happens."

"It's not right." A muscle ticked in his jaw. "I'm filing a complaint. Not against you, but against the decision. Chief Rosen wasn't in his right mind."

"Agreed."

Marshal jerked. "You agree?"

"Yes. I don't want this job. I'd rather be out there ridding the world of scum. The sooner they find a suitable replacement, the better." Pierce peered up at his partner. "You've a demon on your neck."

"Ugh." Marshal swatted at the offensive being. "They're like flies."

"Get rid of the doubt inside you, and they'll go away." Pierce leaned his arms on the desk top. "Are you upset that I'm the new chief, or are you influenced?"

"Maybe a little of both." He pointed at the chair. "May I?"

Pierce nodded.

"Where are our magical partners?"

"No idea." The Glen would be Pierce's first guess, hunting for Kasdeya the second. When Shayna had passed his office, she'd looked more hopeful than when she'd left. "I guarantee they've something up their sleeves." He wasn't sure he'd like whatever it was.

For the next four hours, he took complaint after complaint from officers and staff. It didn't take long for it to become clear that something evil was at play. The amount of demons taking up residence in the precinct were hard to miss. No longer just on the roof, they darted around the offices causing havoc. Grabbing his keys from a dish on his desk, Pierce hurried to his car and headed for Paddy's Pub.

As soon as he entered, he held up his glowing palm. "I've got some questions."

Paddy looked shocked, then nodded. "Come on back. We'll talk somewhere private." He led Pierce to a room behind the bar. "Have a seat. So you've a bit of the blarney."

"A little." Pierce sat in a forest-green vinyl chair. "Shayna and Deema have gone somewhere and the precinct is full of pests. All I can do is cause things to fly through the air and hit its target. Oh, and turn things to gold, which isn't much use in this war. How can I get rid of Kasdeya's minions?"

"Yourself?" He shook his head. "Douse the place with holy water."

"Where can I get it by the bucketful?" Or fire truck. It would take a lot more than the small amount he carried in his pocket.

"You're part leprechaun, and you don't know that all you have to do is have water blessed by a priest to make it holy? Dude." Paddy tilted back in his chair until only the two back legs rested on the floor. "You've a lot to learn."

"It's that easy?"

"Yeah." He glowered. "Get a firetruck, find a priest, get the water blessed, and spray your building. You'll find Father Francis at the bar. The man likes his whiskey, but he's still a priest and easy to find."

"Thanks. Any idea where I can find a barrel of lemon juice?"

"The grocery store?" Paddy glowered. "Now go. I've work to do."

Pierce headed for the bar and peered through the dim room until he found the priest hunched over a glass. He sat across from him at the small round table. "Father, I need your help."

"A lot do, my son."

"No, I mean I need you to bless the water inside of a firetruck tank."

The man lifted bleary eyes. "What?"

"I need a bunch of holy water fast."

"All right. I've nothing better to do." He drained his glass and headed out the door, his black robe rustling around his feet.

Pierce drove the priest to the fire station, distracted the firemen with jokes while the priest blessed the water, then arrested the cleric for hiking up his robe and urinating on one of the tires. His day kept getting better and better.

"I need you to bring the firetruck to the precinct and spray it with all the water in the tank." He grinned at the fire chief.

"Say what?" The man's mouth fell open.

"It's a dare…" Pierce widened his grin.

The fireman shrugged. "Since we don't have a fire at the moment, sure. Weird request, though." He motioned for a couple of firemen to follow the squad car.

After tucking Father Frances into the back seat, Pierce parked in front of the station and filmed as the firemen opened their hoses and sent demons scurrying. Shayna would have loved the sight. She'd have to settle for a video.

When the tank ran dry, Pierce booked Father Frances on drunk and disorderly conduct and put him in a holding cell until morning. Finished, he sat back in his chair, crossed his arms behind his head and felt pretty good about how he'd handled the situation. Did he want Shayna? Oh, yes. Did he need her for every little thing? It didn't appear so. He was a lot more capable at handling things than he'd thought, but it was a lot more fun with her at his side.

"You look pleased with yourself." Payson leaned in the doorway.

"I am. I just rid this entire place of demons. Notice how much better behaved everyone is?"

"As a matter of fact, I do. Good job. Where's Deema? They've been gone a long time." Payson lowered into a chair.

"They have." Worry started to niggle at the edges of Pierce's mind. "We have to trust them."

"I do. With my life, to be exact, but I can't help but worry over how long they've been gone."

18

Shayna

"**We've been walking for** hours." Deema slapped a leafy branch away from her face and glanced over her shoulder. "Are you sure there's a wizard left in these woods?"

"Yes." Not really. Shayna increased her pace. "I'll take the lead."

"How do you know?"

"A gut feeling." More like an intense hope.

Deema groaned. "Seriously, my patience with this hunt is waning. There are other things we could be doing with our time. Like ridding the world of Kasdeya and her minions."

"Hush." Shayna stopped before entering a small clearing. A tiny hut nestled under the far trees. A flower-lined path led to a wooden front door and flowers grew on the thick, grassy roof. Butterflies flitted around the windows. Whoever lived there followed the Light. She smiled. "We're here."

"Looks like a gnome's house." Deema peered around her.

"Be prepared in case it's an enchantment." Shayna put her hand on the hilt of her sword.

They inched forward slowly, their booted feet clomping loud on the cobblestone path. The closer they got to the front door, the more frantic the butterflies grew until they vanished through the front window.

The door creaked open an inch. "Who goes there?"

"Shayna and Deema of The Glen. We've come seeking help."

"Go away. I don't want to get involved."

Shayna cut a quick glance at Deema, then back at the hut. "You know about the war?"

"Yes. Who doesn't? Go away." The door slammed shut.

Shayna knocked on the door hard enough to rattle the frame. "We aren't leaving until you speak to us."

Something smashed against the other side of the door. "Enter at risk of peril."

Shayna shoved the door open and threw up a protective shield in time to deflect a tin teapot hurled at her head. "We're seeking someone with great magical power. Are you a wizard?"

"Wizard, witch, whatever. Yeah, last of my kind, yada yada." A hunched-over old woman of indeterminate age shuffled to the fireplace and poked a stick at the ashes. "Don't expect me to offer you food or drink."

"Wouldn't think of it. May we sit?"

"Suit yourself."

"Sour old thing," Deema muttered.

"My hearing is impeccable, you stupid faerie." The witch circled, green eyes flashing under lowered brow.

"My apologies." Deema looked anything but apologetic as she sat in a cane-backed chair.

Shayna chose a seat next to her. "Kasdeya has released legions of demons on the human world. Radella has joined her and is aggressively converting. Alvar, our most powerful faerie, magic-wise, has joined their side. Do you follow good or evil?"

The witch rolled her eyes. "You think someone who practiced black magic would have butterflies and flowers? Use your brain."

"We need someone more powerful than Alvar, but I think we may have come to the wrong place. I'm sure your magic has waned as your bad temper has grown." Shayna pretended to stand, playing on the witch's pride.

Her eyes narrowed. "There is nothing more powerful than a witch or wizard when it comes to magic, you imbecile."

Shayna exhaled harshly. "Kind words would be more effective here."

"Then you came to the wrong place." She wrapped an inky black robe around her shoulders.

"If the darkness overtakes the human world, the Light is extinguished. Hiding in this forest will not protect you." Shayna crossed her legs.

"Don't come in here in your glittery armor and threaten me." The witch pointed at a lamp and blasted it off the table.

"Your show of power will not frighten me, nor do I lie about the outcome of losing." Her patience started to wear thin. "We have things to do. Will you come and fight with us or not?"

"Who else is on this foolish quest?" She sucked her teeth.

"Sprites, dragons, leprechauns, light and dark-haired faeries…human detectives."

"I don't care for any of those." She held out a finger and smiled as a butterfly landed there. "I like butterflies."

"They aren't much use in a fight."

"Oh, really?" She cackled and whispered something. The butterfly grew to an eight-foot height, bowing under the weight of the hut's roof. "What were you saying, dear?"

Shayna laughed and clapped her hands. "You've enchanted them. What else can they do?"

"Their bite is fatal to the undead. You, unfortunately, can't be harmed." She whispered something else and the butterfly returned to its normal size. "I am a witch of the forest. Anything that makes it home in the woods is under my control." She paced the room, demanding they be quiet so she could think. After several minutes, she took a deep breath and circled toward them. "My name is Agatha. I'll come."

Shayna's grin widened. "With you, we can't lose. I'm Shayna and this is Deema."

"Silly names. Give me time to pack a bag." Agatha picked up a wand from a nearby table, and with a flick, filled a small black bag with too many things to fit under normal circumstances. When she'd finished, Agatha stuck the wand inside her robe. "There. I think I have everything."

"You forgot the kitchen sink," Deema said.

"Why would I need a kitchen sink?" Agatha shook her head. "Let's go. I'll leave my darlings behind. They'll come when I call."

Shayna headed out the door, her steps light. Agatha might be the last of her kind, and grouchy, but Alvar would be no match for her magic. And…having animals cause trouble to the other side during a battle would give those who follow the Light opportunity to diminish a foe while they were occupied with a manic butterfly.

She laughed again, startling birds from the trees. Her instinct had been right, and now they forged through the forest with a grumpy witch at their side.

Radella

"Our numbers have increased by fifty." She bowed in front of Kasdeya. "Not a lot, but every day there are more of us. How long until we battle?"

"Not until I think we have enough fighting on our side." Kasdeya paced, fury on her brow. clearly agitated at how those of the Light kept bouncing back from her attacks.

"Do not fret, my queen." Alvar smiled, toasting the demon with a glass of wine. "I am strong enough."

Her eyes flashed, causing Radella to flinch and retreat. "For what?" her question came out as a hiss. "You couldn't defeat two faeries of the Light with a magical bomb! And now—" She jammed a finger in his chest, "we cannot have spies in the police department. Who told that human to spray the place with holy water?" She spun toward Radella. "Find out and dispose of him or her. Now."

Radella snapped her fingers and left. How in the world of darkness was she supposed to find out that bit of information? Anyone could have told him. She stood in front of the precinct. Not only demons couldn't enter, but she couldn't either, unless invited. That probably wouldn't happen.

She scanned the sidewalks for help. Who would answer her question? Who would know? She shook her head. Senseless waste of time. Only a priest could...she smiled. Father Frances, a regular at Paddy's Pub. That drunk would do just about anything when he'd been drinking. She snapped her fingers and appeared in front of the pub.

No one stood behind the bar, despite the large number of people inside. No matter. She knew where the office was and stormed toward the door.

Paddy sat behind his desk, a large number of silver-tipped items on his desk. "Have you come to play?"

"How did you know I was coming?"

"You aren't the only race with spies everywhere."

She cursed. "You told the human how to protect the police building."

"No, that was our lovely Shayna." He grinned, swirling his finger to cause a knife on his desk to twirl. "I'll count to three before knives start flying. One, two—"

"I'm leaving." She backed toward the door. "My beef is not with you. See you on the battlefield. I'll enjoy spilling your blood." Once outside the door, she grabbed the arm of a passing customer and dragged him into the alley. A feeding would soothe her stress. Kasdeya would not be pleased that the person she most wanted to kill, and so far had failed, had been the one to help the detective.

Pierce

"A witch?" Why did Pierce continue to be shocked with new fairy-tale characters coming to life?

Marshal leaned forward, staring into the old woman's face. "Are gremlins real, too?"

"What's a gremlin?" The witch shoved him back with a wave of her wrinkled hand.

"Goblins?" Payson asked.

"Yes, but they haven't come out of hiding for decades." She sat in a chair, wrapping her cloak around her. "You don't want them to, either."

"This is Agatha, our key to winning the war." Shayna beamed from behind the witch. "She can summon all forest creatures to our aid."

"I don't see how a bunny could do any harm?"

Marshal scowled.

"Maybe not," Agatha said, "But a six-foot bunny could do a lot of damage."

"Everyone, quiet." Pierce held up his hand. "We decided weeks ago to trust Shayna. If she says Agatha is an asset, then she is. What can you do, Miss Agatha?"

She cackled. "I like this one. He has respect. There isn't a lot I can't do, but the greatest power is putting a shield over everyone who fights for us. It can be removed, of course, by someone with the knowledge, but it will give us an upper hand in the beginning so we can get closer to the enemy."

"Closer to the enemy. Great." Marshal poured himself a drink. "Anyone?"

"Me." Seamus appeared in a shower of gold and green sparks. "Agatha, my dear. It's been a long time. You don't look a day over a million years."

"Quiet, you ancient fool, or I'll turn you into a toad." Her smile caused a myriad more wrinkles.

"Make it a green one." He kissed the back of her hand. "Glad you've joined us, but alas, I'm not here with good news."

"What is it?" Pierce asked. He'd hoped for a relaxing evening to share the news of the day's accomplishments.

"Paddy has been targeted because of helping you with the holy water."

"What's this?" Shayna's eyes widened.

Pierce explained about dousing the precinct. "He only told me about Father Frances, not about the holy water. I already knew. What can we do to protect him?"

"Deema, take Paddy to the safety of The Glen until the time to fight has come," Shayna said, laying a hand on Pierce's shoulder. "You did well." She planted a soft kiss on his cheek.

He placed his hand over hers. "Because you've prepared me."

Agatha held up a cross. "No need for him to go away. I've enchanted this. As long as it hangs around his neck, Paddy cannot be touched by Kasdeya or any of her followers." She dropped the necklace into Seamus's hands. "Go in the Light, old friend."

He grinned up at her, downed the shot of whiskey, and disappeared.

"I guess having a witch on our side might be beneficial after all," Marshal said. "Can I get one of those necklaces?"

Agatha pulled a handful of crosses hanging on chains from inside her bag. "Enough for everyone."

19

Shayna

Shayna glanced from the half-empty vial of water to the laughing Deema. When she glanced back at the vial, it had filled again. Still, she feared her friend indulged too much.

"The dark-haired idiot is drunk," Agatha said, disgust filling her words. "Shall I zap her to sanity?"

"It wouldn't do any good. She'll have to be weaned." Shayna sighed and replaced the vial in her pocket. Tonight, she'd sleep with it under her pillow.

"What's wrong?" Pierce wrapped his arms around her from behind and nuzzled her neck. "Any plans for today?"

She nodded, leaning into him. "Deema and I will scour the streets for vampires."

"Without Agatha?"

"We don't want the other side to know about

her until the time to fight." She turned and put her arms around his neck. "Deema is drinking the water."

He pulled back to stare into her face. "What do we do about it?"

"I'll have to wean her. It won't be pleasant for any of us." If Deema thought the test in The Glen had been awful, the weaning would be much worse. Deema would be almost impossible to live with. "It would be easy for me to follow the same path, but after finding Agatha and knowing you can manage a bit without me, a lot of pressure has lifted from my shoulders."

He leaned his forehead against hers. "I love you, Shayna." Without waiting for a reply, he tilted her face to his and kissed her. "Don't answer. Just know that I do. I'll see you later. There's no need to follow me to the station." He pulled the cross from inside his shirt.

"Never take it off."

"I won't." He kissed her again and left, Marshal and Payson following.

"Deema, we have vampires to get rid of." Shayna's words sounded harsh even to her ears. "Then, you and I have other work to tend to."

Deema frowned. "If this is about the water, don't worry about me. I'm fine. I use it to help me relax at the end of the day."

"You aren't fine. You laugh like a hyena," Agatha said. "Bye, girls. Have a good day. I'll be here watching the human television. Great invention. I like the shows where people air their dirty laundry. What a hoot."

Shayna had no idea what she talked about. not understanding the lure of the television. At least the witch would be in hiding while she and Deema worked. Outside, she stood silent and focused on the darkness until she sensed two vampires who had a woman cornered in an alley. She grabbed Deema's hand and teleported.

Two male vampires circled a frightened teenage girl. Laughing, they pushed her from one to the other, acting in no hurry to attack. They stopped at the sight of the faeries. The larger of the two grinned. "Oooh, this will be fun and tasty." He shoved the young girl into a dumpster and shut the lid against her screams.

"Let the girl go." Shayna held her hands at her side. Her palms glowed blue.

Deema did the same, her hands purple. "You can't beat two of us."

He glanced at his partner. "Looks like a fair fight, doesn't it, Roy?"

"Sure does." Roy, a tall lanky vampire flashed his fangs. "I'll take the dark one, Steve. Never been partial to blonds."

Shayna and Deema stood back-to-back as the vampires circled them like buzzards. Shayna kept her gaze locked on the one named Steve. So, they'd be dance partners. She smiled and waved him forward.

He obliged, lunging at her with fangs exposed. She whipped her sword from its scabbard with one hand and zapped him with a blue laser with the other.

He stumbled back a few feet, then charged

again. This time, Shayna met his advance and sank her sword into his chest. "Too easy. These must be new converts and untrained in the skill of fighting."

"Good. The more newbies we get rid of the better."

After freeing the young girl from the dumpster and sending her on her way, Shayna and Deema set off to find more undead to finalize their departure into hell. The vampires were scattered across the city rather than grouping together in a stronger force. Radella definitely focused more on converting than conquering at this point. If Shayna and Deema could rid the world of vampires faster than she could create them, they might cause the dark side to suffer a fatal blow to their plans.

"Stop!" Kasdeya appeared in front of them. Her hands blazed with flames. "I will kill you here and take out all the civilians around us."

Shayna immediately set a shield around her, Deema and the demon. "You cannot win against us alone, but you're welcome to try."

Kasdeya threw a fire ball.

Shayna stumbled back. "You've learned a trick or two." The demon's fire shouldn't have been able to touch her. "Did Alvar teach you magic?"

"Alvar is a good teacher." She grinned.

Shayna blocked the next throw, while Deema kept the shield in place. Pedestrians parted around them like parting waves in a great sea. "I can do this all day."

Kadeya laughed, the sound harsh and without humor. "So can I, little faerie, but don't you have better things to do?"

It was a trick. A trick to pull Shayna away from something, but what? Kasdeya couldn't touch Pierce or the others, not with Agatha's enchantment. She narrowed her eyes at Kasdeya. What was she up to?

"Deema. Teleport." She snapped her fingers and headed back to her apartment.

"Back already?" Agatha brushed cookie crumbs from the front of her robe.

"Kasdeya tried to distract us. We need to figure out why."

"Fine." Agatha pulled a bowl from inside her bag. "The holy water." She wiggled her fingers.

Shayna handed her the water. "You're a fortune teller?"

Agatha glared at her as if she'd gone insane. "Of course not. I do magic, not play games." She poured the water into the bowl, chanted an incantation, and then twirled her finger in the liquid. "Hmmm. She's sent some of her followers to take the mayor."

Pierce

"Why does Kasdeya want the mayor?" Pierce glanced from Shayna to Deema and back to Shayna.

"He's a leader, responsible for making important decisions, is my guess. Let's go." Shayna held out her hand. "We might need the chief-of-police with us this time."

"I'll bring the other two." Deema rushed from

Pierce's office.

He grasped Shayna's hand and landed on the steps of city hall. The sky above them teemed with demons. "Good thing my vial is full." Still holding Shayna's hand, he entered the building. "Police business," he flashed his badge at the guard who tried to stop him from sprinkling the holy water around the door. "We need to speak with the mayor."

"He's in a meeting."

"I don't care." Pierce glared. "We need to speak with him now."

The man clenched his jaw and spoke into his radio. "Fine. Follow me."

"When I shake hands with him," Shayna explained, "he'll be momentarily confused. Dose him with water at that time."

Pierce nodded. "What if his meeting is with one of Kasdeya's people?"

"We'll deal with that if we have to."

Mayor Nichols sat behind his desk alone playing a game on his cell phone when they entered. He stood and greeted Pierce with a handshake. "Chief Cochran, it's a pleasure to meet you. Sorry about Rosen. He was a good man." He raised his eyebrows at Shayna. "Who is this lovely lady?"

She held out her hand. "Special Agent Sky."

When the mayor took the offered handshake, Pierce poured the holy water over his head. "That should do it."

Mayor Nichols frowned, wiping drops from his face. "No idea how I got all wet, but I've a spare shirt in the closet. One moment please." By the time he'd changed and reemerged from his private bathroom, he seemed back to normal. "Please, have a seat. What can I do for you?"

"We're stepping up our fight against gang violence and wanted to know whether we have your support." Pierce grinned. Shayna's touch could work wonders.

"Absolutely. You have my full cooperation and backing." He resumed his seat. "Find out who thinks they're a vampire and lock them up. The people of this city are afraid to go out at night."

"Yes, sir." Pierce grinned in Shayna's direction. "Our thoughts exactly. We'll take our leave now and thank you."

"Any time, Chief." The mayor put a hand on his damp head, clearly confused, then shrugged. "Let me know if there is anything more I can do."

"That was easy," Pierce said as they headed outside.

"Too easy." Shayna frowned at the sky.

The demons hadn't diminished in number, but none perched on the rooftops. A plus in Pierce's mind. "We saved him from influence, just as we wanted."

"I can't help feeling he was nothing more than another distraction."

"For what?"

"I don't know." Her brow creased as Deema, her sword in hand, and his partners appeared. "What took you so long?"

"Vampires had these two surrounded." Deema sheathed her sword. We took care of the three of them, but it wasn't easy. Someone didn't want us here with you."

"We're thinking the same thing," Pierce said. "Coming up empty on the why part, though. Let's head to the station where we can speak in private." He swatted a demon away who flew too close.

Before they could teleport, the swarm descended on them, blocking out the sun and making movement as difficult as sloshing through thick mud. The area between each of them grew larger as the demons increased their number.

"They're trying to separate us." Shayna drew her sword. "Do not let yourself be drawn too far away."

Pierce switched to his armor at the same instant his friends did. To him, it appeared the demons had focused on Marshal and kept pushing him further and further from the group. "Use your water."

"I can't move enough to reach my pocket." Marshal's face paled. "They're too thick."

"You have to stand strong." Pierce fought his way closer. Marshal was the weakest of all of them as far as the Light was concerned. On his own, he wouldn't stand a chance.

When Shayna had space around her, she dropped her sword and emitted a light so bright it blinded him. He froze as the demons rose like a flock of crows. After they'd gone, Shayna collapsed on the sidewalk.

He rushed to her side. "What happened?"

"That spell takes a lot out of me. I'll be fine with rest."

He helped her to her feet. "It worked. Let's get you home. Deema, can you take us?"

She nodded. They held hands in a circle ending up back at the hotel room.

Agatha groaned and switched off the television. "You people interrupt my day too often. What's wrong with blondie?"

"The spell of Light to cast away a horde of demons," Deema explained as Pierce laid Shayna on the bed.

"Move back. Where's that strengthening water?" She patted Shayna down until she located the vial, then fed her a few drops. "That ought to do it. You take a short nap. We'll handle the rest." She frowned at Pierce. "A horde?"

He nodded. "We protected the mayor with holy water, but once Deema and the other two joined us outside, the horde descended. They tried separating us, focusing on Marshal."

Her sharp gaze transferred to his partner. "Why you?"

"I don't know." He sagged into a chair. "It's always me they target."

"Think." She flicked him in the head. "Where does your heart stand?"

"Here, with all of you." He glanced at Pierce. "Tell her."

"He's been with us from day one."

She shook her head. "There's a weakness in him that draws them. Kasdeya knows it. If she can take him, she'll bring him to her side. Where's the necklace?"

He felt his neck. "It must have gotten ripped off in the fight."

"Liar. That isn't possible."

He hung his head. "I took it off to shower and forgot to put it back on."

"If you'd worn it, they wouldn't have targeted you." She threw another necklace at his head. "Don't lose this one. You won't get another."

20

Shayna

Shayna woke fully revived early the next morning and rolled over to face Pierce, his serious gaze locked on her face. "What?"

"I'm watching you sleep, hoping you'd wake up." He gave a sad smile.

"Of course I'd wake up. It was only a spell. I use magic all the time."

"My fear is that someday your eyes won't open."

She caressed his cheek. "Silly man." She kissed him and crawled out of bed to prepare for another day of skirmishes with the undead. Maybe there would never be a big battle if she and Deema rid the city of more vampires than Radella could create. A fae could always hope. She tossed the sheet aside, covering Pierce's face. "Time to get to work."

"Bossy." He slid from bed and dashed past her, flashing a grin. "I get the shower first."

She laughed and waved her hand over her head, cleansing herself without water and changed into her day clothes. She didn't need the shower but did enjoy the feel of steaming water pouring down her back.

While she waited for Pierce, still insisting on accompanying him to the precinct before heading out with Deema, she made coffee, then strolled to the window. What a view. Definitely not as nice as The Glen, but impressive by human standards.

"I'm getting bored." Cup in hand, Agatha joined her. "I can change shape, you know. Anything you want me to be. Then, I could accompany you as a pet." She choked on the last word.

Shayna smiled. "Why not a pigeon? There are so many no one would notice one more."

"You're hilarious. Sure, pick a rat of the sky and think I'd be all right with that."

"Do you have a better suggestion? There aren't many different species wandering the city."

Agatha pursed her lips. "Something small enough to fit into your pocket. Not a mouse. Too many birds to pluck me up. Same with a lizard. How would you feel about having a dog? Forget the pocket idea. A big dog to fight with you. Kasdeya will think you've pulled a shifter over to your ranks."

The idea held merit but carried a lot of risk. "What if you're killed? We need you, Agatha."

"Don't underestimate my strength." High spots of color appeared on her wrinkled cheeks. "I've lived over a thousand years. I doubt my time is coming soon, but if I go into the Light, I'll be fine."

She cackled and patted Shayna's hand. "Stop fretting, child. I'll be here to fight the big battle."

Shayna didn't like it. She also wasn't the witch's boss, just the leading warrior in a battle. She couldn't tell the old woman what to do, so she said, "As you wish."

"Great. I fancy being a rottweiler." She changed, her coffee mug falling to the floor spilling its contents across the carpet. "Ooops." She licked it up until not a spot was left.

"Hey, where'd you get the dog?" Pierce patted its head, jumping back when Agatha snapped. "Whoa."

"It's Agatha. She wants to leave the room and fight."

"Is there anything she can't do?"

"Of course not," Agatha growled. "I'm a witch. Last of my—"

"I know. Last of your kind." He patted her head again and jumped back, laughing. "I hope you're housebroken."

Agatha pounced.

Shayna stepped between them. "Down, girl. He's only joking. You can't be aggressive."

"Right." Pierce laughed. "If you bite, we might have to call animal control."

Heads turned as they entered the precinct with a growling Agatha. Despite Shayna's reprimands, the witch insisted on a show of force, clearly enjoying her role as guard dog.

Marshal slouched in the breakroom. "Where'd you get the mutt?"

Shayna almost told him but put a restraining

hand on Agatha's head instead. "She's a stray. Why are you here so early?"

"Ask the chief. He ordered me to."

"For his protection. Until wearing that necklace becomes a habit, I'm not risking him being taken. Sue me for caring, Marshal." Pierce stepped into his office effectively putting a halt to any further complaints.

When Deema and Payson arrived, they cut a wide swath around Agatha.

"I'll explain later," Shayna said. "Ready?"

Deema nodded. "Is that thing coming with us?"

"Yes." Shayna led the way out of the building. Outside, she said, "It's Agatha. She wanted to leave the room."

"Oh, cool." Deema grinned. "We have a pet."

"I'm beginning to second-guess my choice." Agatha squatted in a patch of grass. "But there are certain liberties to being an animal."

"Dogs do not talk." Shayna led the way to a secluded area and teleported them to Central Park. "I sense several undead here today, and, since we have a dog, where better to walk said pet?" She smiled and turned a fallen stick into a leash. "Sorry, human laws."

After a long walk, she knew the vampires were gone. "What in the world is going on? Nothing is making any sense. There were a significant number of them just moments ago. We're here, basically inviting a fight. Why'd they leave?"

"We need a spy in Kasdeya's penthouse. I'll go." Deema gave a definitive nod.

"She'll kill you."

"Not if I shrink."

"Your power will weaken. You'll be of little use."

"Hey, it works for Agatha. My ears will still work. *Shreank.*" Deema became three inches tall. "I'll be back with news."

Shayna reached out to snatch her. Her fingers caught nothing but air.

Pierce

After two hours of sitting behind the desk, knowing Shayna faced danger and he wasn't there to help, Pierce nabbed his jacket. He couldn't sit there any longer. "Let's go, Payson. Sorry, Marshal."

"Where are we headed?" Payson jogged to catch up.

"No idea. I'm taking a page from Shayna's book and hunting for trouble." He grinned. "Actually, I thought we'd go make sure Paddy is well after his visit with Radella."

"Sounds safe enough."

They parked in front of the pub and entered to the sound of clacking billiard balls and the odor of stale cigarettes. Paddy wiped beer glasses behind the bar. He grinned as they approached and showed the necklace around his neck. "Not a lick of trouble since putting this on. Thanks for the gift. Don't tell me where it came from; I don't want to know."

"Not a problem." Pierce perched on one of the stools. "You haven't seen any demons or vampires?"

"Outside, but they don't bother me. It's wonderful. Where's the faerie?"

"Out walking a dog."

"Again, I don't want to know. Drinks on the house?"

Pierce shook his head. "We're working."

"Looking for trouble is more like it," Payson said. "Our new chief here is going a little stir crazy."

"I can help with that." He leaned close. "There's a gathering of leprechauns taking place near the portal. Seamus is filling them in on what's coming. You should attend."

"They're out in the open?"

Paddy shook his head. "Only fae can see them."

"We will, thanks." It never hurt to know what others were up to, and he'd like to meet more of his kind.

"I'll feel out of place," Payson said when they returned to the car. "You go, and I'll head back to the station. Marshal and I can handle anything that comes in."

"Good idea." The leprechauns might not take kindly to an outsider. Pierce would pose enough of a problem. He tossed Payson the car keys and hailed a cab. When he arrived at the appointed place, the clearing was empty.

Deema

It took a while for Deema to find a way into the apartment. She hid in a silk ficus tree until Radella arrived, then flew in before the vampire could close the door. Keeping low to the ground, she darted to the nearest end table and hopped up into a lampshade.

"It took you a full day to find out who I need to kill?" Kasdeya's gaze would have burned anyone not already dead.

"It was Shayna." Radella stood in front of the demon and lowered her head.

"Of course, it was. I should have known. That fae is a constant source of irritation." Kasdeya paced. "Where's Alvar?"

"I don't know. I assumed he would be here with you."

"Well, he isn't! He never tells me anything. I'm surrounded by insubordinates. My master is quite unpleased." She dropped into a chair and rested her head in her hand. "I need him to teach me more magic. Something that won't leave me as drained as the fireballs do."

"No offense, but you aren't a magical creature. There will be little he can teach you."

A fireball from Kasdeya's hand slammed Radella into the wall, leaving a large hole in the drywall. "Don't tell me what I cannot do, and get that hole fixed."

Radella climbed slowly to her feet. "Whatever you say."

"Don't be insolent."

Deema perched on the lightbulb to regain her strength and smiled. Trouble in the ranks. It was interesting to know Kasdeya wasn't at the top of the food chain after all. This could only be good for their side. Shayna would love hearing that Kasdeya's magic was limited and she was nothing more than a link in the chain of darkness.

Alvar appeared in a shower of silver sparks. "Ladies." He headed straight for the whiskey decanter. "Anyone want to join me?" He glanced at the hole in the wall. "I see the boss is angry again."

"Shut up, Alvar. I need you to teach me more magic. I also need a way to rejuvenate between spells."

"Only so much I can do, my lady. Your kind isn't supposed to have magic."

"My kind?" She blocked his path, hands on her lithe hips. "Regardless, you will teach me what you can or I'll summon every demon at my disposal to finish you."

He sighed and raised a toast. "Of course. Shall we get started?"

"The sooner the better."

He drained his glass and set it on the sideboard. "Use your mind to move that glass. Focus." He twirled a finger around her head.

The glass stayed put. "Focus harder." His finger continued to twirl until the glass moved a fraction.

"Well done. With practice, you may learn to throw things through the air using your mind. The only problem is the spell I did over you will have to be redone on a regular basis. Not always effective during a fierce battle."

She slapped his hand away. "Then show me something else. How do I throw up a shield? If I can't go on the offense, I'll use defense."

"This will require some thought. A few moments, please. We have a visitor." He took the chair next to the lamp where Deema hid.

She held her breath and froze. Any movement would alert him to her presence.

"Would you like to know what astounds me, my lady?"

"What?" Kasdeya narrowed her eyes.

Alvar returned to the sideboard and emptied a vase of its silk flowers. "That a simple little faerie actually believed she could hide undetected when I entered the room." He pointed toward the lampshade.

Deema bolted into the air.

Alvar darted forward scooping her into the vase and covering the opening with his hand. "We have a pet. Isn't she darling?" He set the vase back on the sideboard and set a magical shield over the opening.

21

Shayna

When Deema did not return by morning, Shayna feared the worst. Her friend had been captured or killed. Why wouldn't the headstrong woman listen to her?

"If she would have given me the chance," Agatha said, smoothing her robe, "I could have put an invisibility shield around her that no one other than myself could detect. She's impulsive and a liability. Even more so now that she relies on the water."

"She's a strong warrior."

"Yes, but warriors need more than physical strength. They need discipline, which Deema lacks."

"She'll gain discipline. What she lost while working with Kasdeya will take time to return to her." Shayna refused to give up on her friend.

"We can't leave her there," Pierce said. "What

can we do? Storm the penthouse?"

Shayna shook her head. "Agatha will have to shield me, and I'll go alone. I can handle Kasdeya if Alvar isn't there, regardless of my size."

"You said it would drain you." Pierce shook his head and glanced at Agatha. "Isn't there a way I can go with her?"

"Not unless you know how to make yourself small. You need to realize, chief, that there are some things that not even a part fae can do. I could make you small, I suppose, but there's a great chance you couldn't return to size or would return at an inopportune time. Best you stay here with me."

Shayna would need a way inside without waiting for the front door to open. She needed to make herself small enough to squeeze under the door, which would take even more of her energy. Once inside, she'd use what little she had left to rescue Deema and let the other faerie bring her home. If, and it was a mighty big if, she didn't get caught or killed, too. She planted a kiss on Pierce's lips and shrank to a size smaller than his finger.

"She's too small." His eyes widened. "What can she accomplish at this size?"

"A lot more than you think." Agatha held out her hand. Shayna landed on her palm and stood still as the witch cast a shield over her.

"Wow." Pierce leaned close. "She really is invisible."

"Hurry, my little butterfly. The spell will only last an hour."

Pierce opened the room door and out she flew.

"You'd better come back, Shayna. I can't do this without you."

Although he couldn't see her, she smiled over her shoulder. She'd forgotten the thrill of flying. Shayna patted her pocket to make sure the strengthening water was there. It would give her enough strength for what she needed to do.

It took five minutes of her hour to reach Kasdeya's penthouse and another thirty for Radella and Alvar to leave. The faerie narrowed his eyes and glanced up and down the hall. He must have sensed the presence of a fae but couldn't see her. He shrugged and followed the vampire to the elevator.

Shayna squeezed under the door and hovered in the center of the room. Kasdeya stared out the large window. Deema banged on the glass of a crystal vase. She was alive. Relief flooded through Shayna.

She sent a small spark into the air to let her friend know she was there.

Deema quit pounding.

Shayna took a sip of the water and landed next to the vase. Using all the power her tiny body afforded her, she scooted the vase toward the edge, inch by slow inch. *Oh, please don't die when this shatters.* The vase tipped and fell, breaking into two large pieces.

Unscathed, Deema flew to the sideboard, groped for Shayna's hand, and teleported them away to the sound of Kasdeya's cursing. "That is one unhappy demon," Deema said, laughing. "Alvar was actually going to preserve me in something called resin. After he killed me, of course, as if I were some kind of trophy to display."

"Just get us home. I need to lie down." Shayna's wings could barely hold her. Nausea roiled in her stomach. If not for Deema's tight grip, she'd have fallen to the pavement below.

"We'll both be fine after a drink of that magical water." Once they reached the hotel room, Deema sent a bolt of purple at the door to let those inside know they'd arrived.

Pierce yanked the door open. "She's still invisible."

"Not for long." Agatha motioned for Deema to land on the bed. "You'll both need rest. Shayna will need help returning to her normal size." She blew into her hand. Gold flakes drifted on the air landing on both Shayna and Deema.

Within seconds, Shayna returned to sight and full size, stretched out on the bed for yet another long nap. She held up a hand for Pierce. "Where are you going?"

"To a leprechaun meeting. I showed up yesterday, only to find out it had been postponed because Seamus had too much to drink." He grinned, then kissed her palm. "It's good to see you again."

"It's good to be back." She shifted toward where Deema lay. "Sleep. No water."

Her friend paled. Her smile faded. "Are you serious?"

"Very. You'll heal the way we always heal. You do foolish things, then depend on the water to restore you. That's not how it should be."

"Whatever." She rolled to her side, putting her back to Shayna.

"She'll get over it," Pierce whispered in Shayna's ear. "See you later. Sleep now."

She nodded and closed her eyes. Her body lay heavy on the pillow-top mattress, but she managed a smile. She'd flown into the demon's lair and brought back one of her own. With her strength and Agatha's magic, they could unite their allies and win the war. She no longer harbored any doubt in her mind.

The Light might lose a few fighters during the big battle, but the Light would continue to shine. She'd do everything she could to make sure it happened.

Pierce

Twelve men sat in a circle in front of the portal. Seamus stood in the center, sober, a grave look on his face. "We are gathered here so we can easily escape should our presence be detected."

"Why not hold the meeting in The Glen?" Pierce asked. "If you're afraid of discovery, despite the shield, wouldn't that be safer?"

"It would, but…well, I had a misfortunate accident once after imbibing too much of the faerie wine, and the queen and I—"

Pierce laughed. "Understood."

"There's not a fae in this world or the other that does not know of the coming battle. I'm going to Ireland this very day to bring back fighters. We will stand with the faeries. We will fight with our last breath, if we must. We will stop the darkness."

Cheers rose at his inspiring speech. Pierce couldn't help but think what a great leader the little man was and entertained the idea of making him the new chief someday. He thought better of it when Seamus pulled a flask from his pocket. Still, he didn't doubt the man's words or enthusiasm and cheered along with the others.

"We have the dragons on our side!" Seamus raised his flask. "The pesky sprites and faeries! We'll have armor covered with dragon scales." Voices cheered louder.

Pierce wasn't sure whether it was true about the armor, but if anyone could make it happen, it would be Shayna. He'd mention it to her when he returned to the hotel.

A crashing through the bushes sent them scrambling through the portal. Squeezing through as a large group had its disadvantages. Instead of walking, chaos ensued as they stumbled over one another, to the amusement of several faeries.

Earin peered down at them. "What do we have here? Uninvited leprechauns?"

"We came to avoid detection." Seamus struggled to his feet and straightened his emerald green vest. "We'll turn right around and leave."

The faeries froze, then bowed as Queen Linette approached. "There is no need of that. Come with me and stay away from the wine, my small friend."

Pierce choked back a laugh, then sobered. What could the queen want with them? "Is she the queen of all fae?"

Seamus shook his head, "No, but respected by all races. It doesn't do anyone any good to thwart her. Her guard is heavily armed with fierce warriors."

The queen led them to her royal chamber and took a seat on her crystal throne. Pierce and the others bowed. "Rise, my friends. Refreshments will be served shortly. Now, what brings you to The Glen?"

Pierce cut a glance at Seamus who motioned for him to proceed. He swallowed against the sudden lump in his throat. Things looked a lot different without the queen's favorite warrior at his side.

"Seamus called a meeting to inform everyone about what is going on in the human world. He's leaving later today to gather more forces from Ireland."

"Don't forget the armor," Seamus whispered, elbowing him in the side.

Pierce frowned. "And he'd like dragon armor for all the leprechauns." He lowered his eyes.

"That is not for me to decide," the queen said. "The dragons usually only give scales to those they favor. Leprechauns are not favored."

"My lady." Seamus bowed. "We no longer create the mischief we once did. With your confidence, the dragons are sure to approve us. Properly outfitting us benefits all who fight."

"I will see what I can do. Now, everyone except Chief Cochran move to the dining hall. He and I will join you in a few minutes." She waved a hand in dismissal. When the others had left, she turned to Pierce. "I have learned that Shayna visited the dragon's pool."

"Yes."

"Why?"

He explained about the bombing and the loss of life. "She'd lost hope, but now she's stronger than before."

"Does she carry the water with her? If let into the wrong hands, the favor of the war would turn to the dark."

He took a deep breath and squared his shoulders. The queen wouldn't be pleased with his next words. "After finding out that Deema had gotten into the water, it no longer leaves Shayna's possession."

"Although Deema's powers grow stronger with each day she follows the Light, she is not strong enough to resist some things. I'm glad Shayna realized that before too much time has passed." She stood and held out her hand. "Come. Let's dine and fellowship with our friends."

He escorted her to a large marble room. A table, long enough to accommodate twenty diners, stretched across the middle of the room. Three tables laden with food lined one wall, a fourth on the opposite wall held drinks.

Seamus caught the queen's eye and set down the glass of red liquid. "I almost gave into temptation."

She laughed and took her seat at one end of the table, motioning for Pierce to sit on her right in representation of Shayna. Earin sat on her left. She clapped her hands. "Please, fill your plates with my blessing. I am thrilled to spend time with friends."

Seamus's group stampeded to the buffet,

leaving Pierce to wait until the line shortened. "Thank you for not removing an eye that first day."

Her laugh was almost as musical to his ears as Shayna's. "I sensed the fae in you, Chief. In my heart I knew Shayna had chosen wisely. You are free to come and go from the realm as you please. The portal will never be closed against you."

Gladness coursed through him. No matter what Shayna's decision when the battle was won, he'd follow her until she agreed to bind herself to him or told him he had no chance. While he waited to eat, he filled the queen in on Deema's latest escapade, expecting her to request he bring the stubborn faerie to her.

"I'm certain Shayna can handle Deema's waywardness." A smile graced her lips. "Withholding the water from someone addicted is tough on the one addicted. Although," her eyes twinkled, "by the time it's over, you will all wish Deema could take a small sip."

Great. It sounded like being around someone who tried to quit smoking. "May I fill you a plate?" Pierce stood and gave a slight bow.

"You may. A little of everything, please."

He joined the line and stared at food he didn't recognize. Red food, green food, blue food…it all looked the same except for the color and smell. Relying on his nose for familiar smells, he filled his plate and the queen's.

His first bite told him he should have followed her example and gotten some of everything. He'd never tasted anything so delicious. Nor had he ever felt as satisfied after eating. He could grow accustomed to life in The Glen.

"Don't tell the leprechauns just yet," the queen whispered. "I enjoy letting Seamus worry. The dragons will gladly give scales for armor. They know the need."

Pierce laughed and kept eating.

22

Shayna

"*If I win, you give* me a drink." Deema lunged.

Shayna parried, her sword driving the other faerie back. "You will not win." She grinned. "I'm the best warrior, remember?"

"But if I…" Deema spun like a dust devil, stirring up the snow at their feet. The flakes drifted like a white fog.

"Couldn't you have found somewhere warmer to fight than Mount Everest?" Pierce shivered. "Your dome may give us the oxygen we need, but it doesn't supply enough warmth."

Shayna laughed and leaped over Deema's head, bringing her sword down on empty space as her opponent ducked and rolled. "If you trained, you'd be warm."

"I'm too frozen to fight, but all right." Pierce drew his sword and turned to his partners. "Let's do this."

The air rang with the sound of clanging swords. Agatha sat on a snowdrift, not appearing the least bit chilled, and read a book on how to be a better person. Something Pierce had suggested the last time some not-so-nice words left the witch's mouth.

Deema's sparring grew more frantic as time passed. Her hands shook, her lunges grew more uncoordinated. Shayna wanted to go easier on her friend, but that wouldn't be beneficial in the end. Maybe if she occupied her mind. "What did you find out while trapped at Kasdeya's?"

"That… she isn't…the boss." Deema fell to her knees. "A minute, please. I meant to tell you when I returned, but we went straight to bed."

"Get up. You cannot take a break. What if the battle came today? You have to push through your need and fight as if your life depends on it, because soon it will." Shayna held the tip of her sword under Deema's chin and tilted her head to face her. "If not Kasdeya, then who rules?"

Deema struggled to her feet. "I don't know."

"Is Abaddon real?" Payson shouted, circling Pierce. "Since most creatures are more than part of human fables, then perhaps he is too. In mythology, he's the demon of destruction, the chief of the underground."

Shayna's hand stilled just enough for Deema to swipe her sword, knocking Shayna off her feet. She stared at the crystal blue sky overhead. Could it be true? She'd never known any other name but Kasdeya's in regard to controlling the dark minions.

"Are you all right?" Deema plopped next to her,

her breathing heavy and shuddering. She lay back into the snow. "I need a sip, Shayna. Just a small one. I can't focus on anything else."

Shayna sat up and wrapped her arms around her knees, her gaze on the men. "No. We need to find out who is the leader of darkness. If we kill him, then we'll prevent a battle."

"You can't kill him." Pierce sat next to her. "You need to find a way to bind him, using light, I think. Payson and I will have to study on it more."

"We must find him." Shayna sighed. "I doubt he'll be at the battle, if he even exists."

"Too bad we can't ask Kasdeya." Deema clenched her fists. "Give me a drink." She climbed to her feet. "I won our skirmish."

"I didn't make that deal." Shayna met her angry glare.

Deema's palms glowed purple.

Shayna's blue. "You don't want to do this."

"It's your fault." Deema shot a laser. "Just a sip would fix things."

Shayna dove to the side and returned fire. The bolt caught Deema in the chest. She flew in the air, landing hard on her back in the snow.

With a cry of rage, she bolted to her feet and shot with both hands.

"Ladies." Payson jumped between them.

Deema's bolt hit him. He stiffened, then fell like a plank.

"Oh, no." Shayna knelt next to him and stared up at her friend. "Our magic is not meant to be used on humans. I don't have the skill to heal him." The man's cold body lay as if he were dead, hard and unmoving.

Tears coursed down Deema's cheeks. "I'll take him to The Glen. Our queen will heal him. I know she will."

"He's human. You cannot take him."

Deema grabbed Payson's hand. "I have no other choice. I'll beg the queen to be merciful." She locked gazes with Shayna. "I'll trade my life for his if I have to."

A dark shadow passed over the dome. "Uh, people, you might want to stop your bickering and pay attention to what's happening." Agatha pointed at the sky. "It's coming, and coming fast."

Shayna glanced up as the darkness thickened. "It's time to prepare. Make haste, Deema. A battle is coming. We need every fighter we can get." She grabbed the hands of Pierce and Marshal and teleported back to the hotel.

Deema

With her strength low because of her need for the water, Payson's weight lay heavy on her shoulders. Holding her head as high as possible despite the discomfort, Deema ignored the stony glares sent her way and moved as fast as she could to the queen's throne room.

She lay Payson at the queen's feet. "Your mercy on him, please." She raised burning eyes to her queen. "I threw a fit because of my strong desire for the water, and he was zapped with a bolt meant for Shayna. Forgive me and heal him." She prostrated herself on the cold marble floor.

"Rise, Deema." Queen Linette moved to her side. "You care for this man?"

"Shayna charged me with his safety. I take that role seriously." She stood. "I've failed. I know the penalty for bringing a human to our world. Punish me, not him."

"Silence." Queen Linette summoned one of her guards. "Take him to the infirmary."

The guard lifted Payson and dashed away to the sound of swords as fighters trained outside the throne room.

"The darkness is coming. I feel it." Queen Linette put a hand on Deema's shoulder, reviving her strength. "We need our warriors. Is this man a fighter?"

"Yes, my queen. Trained by myself and Shayna."

"Hmm. How many more humans know your true self?"

"One. We've trained the three detectives because of their deception."

She smiled. "You have regained the truth, Deema, and for that I removed your addiction. You've learned a valuable lesson."

"I have." She exhaled heavily. "I could have killed a friend. May I ask you a question?"

"Anything."

"Is Abaddon real?"

The queen flinched. "Where did you hear that name?"

"The man in the infirmary when I told them Kasdeya was not the true boss of darkness." She explained what she had heard when hiding in the demon's room.

The queen swished her gown and paced. "He is the king of the abyss. Leader of darkness. He was chained a millennium ago." She stopped and whirled back to face Deema. "If he escaped his chains, things are far more dire than I knew."

Dread chilled Deema's blood. "Can he be rechained?"

"Yes, but it takes a long time to forge the chains we need. Make haste, Deema. Get your friend from the infirmary and go. I must alert all those who follow the Light. We will gather at the Absaroka Mountain Range this very evening. A battle there will lessen the risk of human casualties." She hurried through a side door, leaving Deema standing alone.

Payson was sitting on a bed piled high with pillows when Deema entered the infirmary. "What in the world happened?"

Deema hung her head. "You were caught in a fight between me and Shayna. I beg your forgiveness."

"Hey, I finally got to visit your world, sort of. Haven't seen anything but this room, but there's nothing to forgive." He grasped her hand. "Ready to take me home? I hear there's a fight coming."

Pierce

"You're all right." Pierce grabbed Payson in a hug when he appeared with Deema. "With both eyes."

"What?" Payson drew back.

"Nothing." Pierce laughed. "It's good to see you."

"The queen said Abaddon is real." Deema sat on the edge of the bed. "He's been chained for a long time and must have escaped or been freed. She's bidden us to meet our allies on the Absaroka Mountain Range today."

"Wyoming?" Pierce frowned. "Why there?"

"Less human life at risk."

Pierce hoped the leprechauns would get their armor in time. He took a deep breath. The time they'd prepared for and feared had arrived. His hands shook. "So, we go there and wait?"

Shayna nodded. "It's a good thing. Our allies will be arriving and plans need to be made." She brushed her hand across his back as she passed. "You're ready, Pierce."

He didn't feel ready. Sure, he had armor, weapons, and a smidgeon of magic, but against a horde of demons and undead? No, he could never feel ready for that. His partners looked as shocked as he felt.

Agatha had been hunched over a bowl the entire time they'd been back and finally straightened. "My creatures are on their way."

"Creatures?" Marshal raised his eyebrows.

"Think Noah's ark, but much bigger." She gave her snaggle-toothed grin. "Just don't try to pet any of them."

"I wouldn't dream of it." Marshal slid another silver-tipped dagger into his belt. "I think that makes ten. Hope it's enough."

"Give me your knives. All of you." Agatha pointed to the sideboard. "Hurry up. We should have done this sooner."

They hurried to do her bidding. She chanted an incantation. "There. They will return to you once thrown, even if imbedded in an enemy. Anything else we need to enchant?" Her gaze roamed over each of them head-to-toe. "No? Then you're as prepared as you can be. Very little will get through that armor."

"It's useful having a witch around." Pierce tossed her a wink.

"No one better than me." Her cheeks darkened. "If I were a thousand years younger, we could be a thing. A witch doesn't follow silly rules of binding like the faeries."

"It's our way." Shayna frowned. "We've no time for such things anyway. Agatha, do you have shelter in your bag?"

"Of course. I'm not an idiot." She slung the strap of her purse over her shoulder. "Are we going to stand around and yak all day or head to the range? I want to get a good spot to set up camp. If we dawdle, we'll end up hanging off the side of a cliff."

"Have I ever mentioned I don't like heights." Pierce glanced around the room. "I'm okay on solid ground, but I can't hang off anything. Remember my flight on your winged horse?" He set his gaze on Shayna.

"I remember." She smiled. "I'll make sure you're on flat ground with no view of anything more than five feet." She held out her hands. "Shall we?"

They held hands in a circle and landed on a plateau in Wyoming.

23

Shayna

Shayna tripped over a bunny on her way to the queen's tent. Animals roamed in and around every solid object making it difficult to walk easily from one spot to another. Agatha refused to make them larger until the time came. While it would make things more crowded with a bigger size, at least a body would know where they were.

She pulled aside the tent flap and stepped into opulence, white silk and fur everywhere as befitted a queen.

Seamus stood on a chair in front of Queen Linette, putting him at eye level with her. "Well, when is the armor coming? I will not send my people into battle without armor. We are two hundred strong. You need us."

"The dragons will arrive by nightfall, fully prepared to outfit your fighters." The queen rarely looked rattled, but today her eyes flashed and her hands shook. "You're the tenth person to complain about something today. We're all doing the best we can, Seamus." She leaned closer to him, a sly smile on her face. "I've asked that your armor be enchanted so you cannot drink whiskey while wearing it. We cannot have you incapacitated during battle. When this fight is over, I'll buy you a vat of whiskey if you want. One large enough for you to swim in."

"You mean to drown me, you evil woman." He hopped down and stormed from the tent.

"Thank the Light, a friendly face." Queen Linette smiled and beckoned Shayna forward. "Please tell me you are not here with a complaint."

"No, my queen, only to make a request and to form a battle plan."

"Good. Join me at the map. Earin is late. You can fill him in when he arrives." The queen moved to a large table with a Wyoming map spread over it. "Your request?"

"That Agatha corral her critters. They're a nuisance at such a small size."

"I will speak with her, although I have no authority over her." She directed Shayna's attention to the map. "Since most of our fighters do not have the ability to fly, I'd like to focus the majority of the battle here." She circled a plateau.

"How will we draw them to that location?"

"I will be there, thus they will come. What better victory than to take the queen?"

Shayna's eyes widened. "You cannot take that risk, my queen."

"Of course, I can. Nothing can touch me, I

assure you. Not with my warriors surrounding me."

"Your safety depends on us?"

She smiled. "I trust no one more."

Earin entered the tent, casting a wary glance at Shayna. "My queen, Shayna. My apologies for being late. A minor skirmish among some tiny wolves."

"I was letting Shayna know my warriors will be responsible for keeping our enemies from me. I will fight alongside you but must not be taken."

"My queen!" Shayna jerked. "You said you could not be taken."

"I said I could not be harmed." The queen's features hardened. "I will have no dispute on this. It is imperative we draw the forces to us rather than let them scatter us. We are stronger as a unified front."

"I'd rather not work alongside leprechauns," Earin said. "Send them to the outskirts."

"We will have no racism here. We fight for a common cause." Her eyes flashed. "Now leave me. The two of you have battle plans to draw up." The queen marched back to her throne.

"That was an idiotic thing to say." Shayna faced Earin outside. "What do you have against them?"

"The fact you would rather bind yourself to one of them than to me." Hurt flickered in his dark eyes.

"That was a decade ago." Shayna took a step back. "You should find another and move on. One who will return your affections."

He grabbed her by the arm. "I don't want another. I have always wanted you."

She pulled free. "Stop. We must not fight. We have to stand together on this."

"Is everything all right?" Pierce approached. His street clothes no longer showed over his armor. He looked so much like a warrior that Shayna's heart skipped a beat. She'd fooled herself for too long. Fae or human, the man had her heart.

"All is fine. Queen Linette has commanded that Earin and I draw up battle plans. We will be in charge of her protection during the battle."

"Really?" His brows rose. "She intends to fight?"

Shayna and Earin nodded in unison. "Our kind do not send others to fight when they are not willing." Earin lifted his chin. "Unlike some races."

"Look, dude. I don't know what that chip on your shoulder is about," Pierce said, "but I'm not getting into a show of testosterone with you. There are more important things to do. Shayna, Agatha said something worrisome is coming on the wind."

Shayna glanced at Earin. "You might as well come." She raced for their tent.

On the outside, the tent looked shabby and took up little space, but on the inside it contained a four-bedroom house complete with kitchen and bathroom. The little witch really was amazing.

Agatha bent over a sink full of bubbles. "Look at this."

Shayna glanced in. "Dirty dishes?"

"No. See how they ebb and flow? Our opponent is growing at an alarming rate and will strike as darkness settles on the mountain." She glanced up. "Where are the rest of our allies?"

"They'll be here." They'd promised.

Shayna drew Earin and Pierce to a table where

her own map of the mountain range lay. "This is where the queen wants to draw our enemy. We will circle her here. The dragons will guard from the air. I want to put our allies in fighting circles like this." She drew different circles with assorted colors, getting smaller as they neared where the queen would stand.

"This will be Agatha's giant creatures." She pointed at the yellow circle, the largest and the first defense against the dark fighters. "Then the sprites and leprechauns, then us faeries."

"I'll fight with Seamus and the others," Pierce said. "Where will Payson and Marshal be?"

"Anywhere they want," Earin said. "They're expendable."

"No, they are not." Shayna glared up at him. "They will fight at our side."

Earin rolled his eyes. "You're too soft to lead troops."

"Yet our queen has every faith in my ability." Shayna huffed and returned to the map. "Our enemy will most likely attack in groups, trying to draw us apart as they did outside the mayor's office. We cannot let that happen."

"We're here." A blue sprite no larger than a cat flew through the tent's opening. "The sky is thick with demons. We had to take the long way around to arrive."

"Did you lose anyone?"

"Three. They chose to lead a large group of demons away in order for us to get through their ranks. The dragons arrived behind us and took care of a lot of the enemy, but there are more than we could count."

Gorna's large head appeared through the tent opening.

"You're here." Shayna wrapped her arms around the dragon's snout. "It's kind of you to armor the leprechauns. They won't forget."

"Ride with me. We need to scout." Gorna withdrew.

"I'll return. See whether there are any holes in my plan. Play nice, Earin." She flashed Pierce a grin and darted outside to climb on Gorna's neck.

"I will fly high enough to keep you safe, but low enough so you can see the enemy's size. It's quite formidable." Gorna flapped her wings, threatening to topple several tents from their force, and flew into the air.

The enemy gathered on the other side of a snow-covered peak, numbering in the tens of thousands, the air over them inky black with demons. A few flew at Shayna and Gorna only to be turned to ash by the dragon's breath, the only fire that could destroy them.

"Filthy pests. They are no challenge for us." Gorna turned. "Look at what you've gathered."

Shayna gazed down upon a score of Light followers. The plateau teemed with armor in every hue of the rainbow. Agatha's giant creatures stood feet above the other warriors. Blue sprites darted here and there in the thousands.

Tears sprang to Shayna's eyes. She'd done it. She'd gathered an army worthy of the Light.

Pierce

"We're on the same side." Pierce crossed his arms. "What do you have against me?"

"You've somehow convinced Shayna to leave her people for you." Earin turned to leave.

"Hold on." Pierce clapped a hand on his shoulder. "What do you mean? She's not said anything about leaving."

Earin whirled, his face inches from Pierce's. "I asked her to bind with me years ago. Now, she's on the edge of doing that very thing with you. A human," he spit the word out.

Pierce stepped back. "She's not said anything like that to me." He tried but couldn't hold back a grin. Shayna cared more for him than she'd let on. After they won this war, he'd make her talk to him, make her declare her love.

"I could kill you."

"And alienate Shayna forever. What's the penalty for murder in your world?" Pierce rubbed his chin. "I'm guessing it's death."

"Take care you don't die on the battlefield." Earin stormed from the tent.

Pierce turned to Deema. "Can he kill me?"

"No." She sneered and shook her head. "He's only trying to intimidate you. The queen would know if you fell at the hands of a faerie."

"What if he gets someone to do it for him?" An icy fist clenched his heart.

"Same thing. The only way you can be killed without repercussions is if you fall at the hands of the enemy." She rose to her feet. "I need to find Payson and Marshal. They should rest."

"Don't worry." Agatha's knitting needles clacked. "I'll turn into a rottweiler and fight at your side. They'll know there's a witch among you when they see my fur babies, but they'll just think I'm another one of the forest creatures. I'll be quite large this time."

He laughed. "You are the strangest person I've ever met."

"You do know how to flatter a girl." She held up a royal blue scarf. "This is for you when I finish. You can wear it the next time Shayna takes you to a mountaintop."

Pierce plopped down in a chair across from her. "Provided there'll be a next time."

She leaned over and knocked him in the head. "None of that kind of talk. Of course, there'll be a next time. We are not a group of losers, Mr. Chief."

He knew that, but knowing and beating a formidable foe were two different things. He would not falter during the battle, he hoped, but he did fear dying at the hands of evil and losing the opportunity of a future with Shayna.

As if his thoughts made her appear, Shayna burst into the tent and wrapped her arms around his neck. "I've seen the enemy."

He pulled her close. "And yet you're smiling. Are there many?"

"Thousands upon thousands."

His heart lurched. "More than we have?"

"Oh, yes, but the majority of their fighters are demons. Not much of a force against the power of the Light." She peered into his face. "We will win this."

He lowered his head to kiss her, murmuring, "Give me a dose of your confidence."

She laughed, making his heart leap. "You may have it all."

The clearing of Agatha's throat pulled them apart. "You're being summoned, dear."

Pierce spun to see Earin glaring from the tent opening. "Go. I'll see you on the battlefield."

"Yes. You must rest. The fight will last a long time." Shayna caressed his cheek and left with Earin.

"Don't worry about a jealous faerie," Agatha said. "It's you who has Shayna's heart."

He hoped so. He lay on his cot, fully clothed, and closed his eyes. He doubted sleep would come, but his body did need rest for the night ahead. He didn't rouse when his partners entered and lay upon their own cots, but he pretended to sleep so they wouldn't involve him in a conversation.

"I'm scared," Marshal admitted. "Me. Tough Luke Marshal of foul mouth and a hard heart is frightened out of his wits."

"You'd be stupid not to be afraid," Payson said. "Close your eyes. Empty your mind. Night will come fast."

Pierce couldn't agree more.

24

Shayna

The ground trembled under their feet as five giants led hundreds of vampires toward them. The air teemed with demons, blocking light from the moon and stars, blocking vital oxygen with their stench.

"Giants?" Shayna glanced back at the queen. "I thought they were extinct."

"So did I." The queen called to the dragons. "Destroy them."

The flapping of seven pairs of wings filled the air as Gorna and the other dragons took to the sky. Demons immediately surrounded them, hindering their flight. Sprites ascended to the dragon's aid, creating a blue cloud and darted among the demons with darts of silver lasers.

"Do not fall back," Shayna cried. "Hold ranks." She'd lost sight of Pierce, Agatha at his side, the moment the demons blocked light. She gripped her sword and prepared to defend the queen.

With massive clubs, the giants swept allies away. Fighters for the Light fell in scores. "Stop those giants!" Shayna motioned for several ten-foot bunnies to move forward. Three giant grizzly bears joined them. "Focus on their ankles. Make them fall, then finish them."

Radella led a pack of vampires who broke off from the main rank to circle around Shayna's warriors. As if one body, the faeries turned, keeping the vampire in their sights.

Four giants fell under the onslaught of giant animals and dragon fire. One burst free and thundered toward the last lines of defense, tossing leprechauns as if they were nothing more than stuffed toys. Bolts of lightning flashed from Seamus's hands as he rushed the giant, Pierce at his side.

Shayna's heart leaped to her throat. Everything in her wanted to go to Pierce's side. She glanced again at her queen and held her ground. Her duties lay here.

While Seamus distracted the giant by showering him with gold, Pierce ducked between the giant's legs and hacked at his ankle. With a cry of rage, the giant turned, exposing his other leg. Another hack and the giant fell. The ground shuddered as a giant fell, narrowly missing a group of allies.

Gorna, bleeding from a wound under one wing, blew fire, cutting a wide swatch through the approaching vampires before turning back to deal with the demons. The vampires who managed to break through raced toward the faeries with swords drawn.

The air rang with the clash of swords and battle cries. "Do not let them in." Shayna sent a blue bolt directly to the chest of a vampire. As the creature stumbled back, she moved forward, piercing him with her sword. For every one she turned to ashes, three more advanced.

She unwound the silver rope at her waist and twirled it, slicing through the undead like butter, leaving them in pieces on the battlefield. "Finish them!"

Marshal and Payson darted forward throwing knives into the undeads' chests before ducking back behind the protection of the faeries.

Radella slid through before the fae could regroup and made a beeline for the queen. She flashed a grin at Shayna and leaped.

Shayna flung the rope. It entwined around the vampire's body, pinning her arms to her side. Radella fell to the ground with a thump and a curse. Before Shayna could move forward, demons descended in a dark cloud. The dragons couldn't help at this point. Not without risking the lives of those being swarmed.

Deema moved from the outskirts of the faerie circle and stood at Shayna's side. Earin took up rank on her other. They would be the last defense in keeping the queen safe.

Deema grinned. "This is a battle worth dying for."

"You're insane." Shayna returned her smile and sliced through a demon darting toward her head.

"Winning isn't as easy as I thought it would be,"

Earin said. "If they hadn't had giants…" He bolted a demon into the air. When it flew back, he shoved his sword through its middle. "These demons are like flies."

"Anyone spotted Kasdeya?" Shayna lunged forward, halting the forward progression of a demon the size of a black bear.

"If she's here, she isn't fighting," Deema said. "My guess is she's directing her fighters from the top of a mountain peak."

Dawn kissed the horizon and still the battle raged. Shayna passed her vial of dragon water among her comrades. As each drank, the bottle refilled.

Deema shook her head, then shrugged. "The queen healed me of my addiction. My strength is waning. I'd be a fool not to drink." She downed the contents in one gulp and handed the vial to another.

Shayna wished the non-faerie fighters could have the same advantage. Weariness slumped their shoulders. The swipe of swords slowed. Even Agatha's remaining creatures moved more slowly. Something needed to happen to shove the enemy back so Shayna's fighters could regroup.

Pierce

The sword grew heavier and harder to wield with each approaching foe. Agatha fought at Pierce's side, biting the heads off vampires stupid enough to get too close. She grinned up at him revealing silver-tipped canines. He laughed. A very clever witch.

"Your hand," she growled.

He obliged. She licked the small amount of skin showing between the glove and sleeve of his armor. Strength coursed through him, reviving him to continue fighting. "Everyone needs their own personal witch."

She laughed and dashed forward to attack another foe before whirling back to him. "I must leave you and revive those I can. Be careful, my friend. Those barrels of lemon juice you think you hid in your tent were a waste of time. Creatures like Alvar don't fight."

He nodded, his smile fading, and backed closer to the fighting leprechauns. He flicked knife after knife at the approaching swarm with one hand and caught them returning on the other. He only had two of his original ten knives, having shared with his fellow fighters.

The enemy continued to advance, driving the surviving warriors for the Light back into a cluster where they were quickly surrounded. Pierce stumbled back, tripping over a bound Radella. He glared and kicked her in the side before raising his sword to ward off an attack.

"We need the Light," Queen Linette cried. "Shayna!"

Pierce whipped around. "No. She'll fall."

"We need it." The queen backed up, her fighters closing in around her. "There's no other way." With a flash of lightening, she disappeared.

"What? She's left us?"

"She goes to prepare for the surviving wounded." Earin stepped in front of Shayna. "Do it now. I'll hold them off."

Pierce's heart stopped in his chest as Shayna sheathed her sword and lifted her hands to the sky. She cast him a sad glance and emitted a light so strong every living and undead creature fell to their knees. She kept her hands high until her legs trembled. The demons fled, leaving behind only the undead.

Pierce rushed forward, hoping to catch her before she fell.

Radella kicked out a leg, knocking Shayna to the ground. Before Shayna could rise, Radella sank her teeth into her neck.

"Shayna!" Pierce thrust his sword through Radella's chest and fell next to Shayna. "What do I do?"

"Get…me…home."

He gathered her in his arms. They were so far away. Deema fought on the other side of the group of faeries. Several vampires surrounded Earin. Pierce raced for a clear spot in the center of the plateau. "Gorna!"

The dragon's massive head swung his way. Her golden eyes widened. "Come," she hissed, lowering her head.

He lay Shayna on the ground and climbed onto the dragon's back. Gorna scooped Shayna into her claws and flew into the air.

Pierce wrapped his arms around a dragon spike, closed his eyes, and held on with all his might. He didn't know how long it took to arrive in Central Park. Nor did he care how many drunk people flew in terror at the sight of Gorna. He retrieved Shayna from the dragon and stepped through the portal.

The halls were strangely silent as Pierce hurried for the throne room only to find it empty. Where was the queen?

He darted through a door and into a garden, Shayna growing heavier with each passing minute. A child faerie peered at him from under the petals of a large flower. "Please, where is your queen?"

The child pointed to a smaller building on their right.

Pierce raced in that direction, barging through the door and into what appeared to be a medical clinic. Queen Linette sat on a cot while a faerie in white stitched a wound in her shoulder.

She glanced up as Pierce entered. "I know I said I couldn't be harmed, but that was to keep my fighters fighting. What happened? Summoning the Light should not have made her that weary."

"Radella bit her." He lay Shayna on a cot. "Please tell me you can save her."

"We can." The queen pushed the nurse's hands away. "Care for her. My wound is not as important."

The queen lied. "What happened to you?" he asked.

"Radella had a poisoned blade. She threw it just as Shayna bound her. I'll be fine." She lay back and closed her eyes. "That is why I had to leave. I needed an antidote immediately."

"Did you receive it?" He stepped back as a

second nurse joined the first in draining the blood in Shayna's neck. "What are they doing to her?"

"They will have to drain her blood, then give it back once it is cleansed. Yes, I received the antidote. Both my best warrior and I will be here for a few days. How goes the battle?"

"The Light forced the demons to retreat." He closed his eyes against the memory of a battle field full of fallen from every race. "The others were quickly finishing the remaining vampires. We won." But at what cost?

He fell asleep next to Shayna's bed after tortured hours of watching her drained of blood and refilled. Exhaustion caught up to him despite his vow to remain alert. He woke to a soft touch on his hand.

Opening his eyes, he gazed into the smiling face of Shayna. "You live." Tears sprang to his eyes.

"I promised, didn't I?"

"You did." He leaned down and kissed her, more grateful than he could ever express. "We won. Reports have been arriving for hours."

"How many did we lose?"

"A lot, but we'll survive to fight again."

She closed her eyes. Before she drifted to sleep again, he swore she'd whispered the words, "I love you."

Stay tuned for book two, Deema. The fight isn't over yet. Keep reading for the first chapter.

Shayna

Dear Reader,

I hope you've enjoyed my foray into Urban Fantasy romance as much as I loved writing it. I fell in love with Shayna the moment I dreamed her up. My hope in writing this was to show the fight between good and evil exists and how those from different walks of life can band together to form a better world.

Thank you for spending time with my friends.

Cynthia Hickey

Shayna

Website at www.cynthiahickey.com

Multi-published and Amazon and ECPA Best-Selling author Cynthia Hickey has sold over a million copies of her works since 2013. She has taught a Continuing Education class at the 2015 American Christian Fiction Writers conference, several small ACFW chapters and RWA chapters. She and her husband run the small press, Winged Publications, which includes some of the CBA's best well-known authors. She lives in Arizona with her husband, one of their seven children, two dogs, one cat, and three box turtles. She has nine grandchildren who keep her busy and tell everyone they know that "Nana is a writer".

Connect with me on FaceBook
Twitter
Bookbub
Sign up for my newsletter and receive a free short story
www.cynthiahickey.com

Follow me on Amazon

1

Deema

The battle a few days ago had dispelled some of the darkness encroaching on the human world, but not enough to restore the day to its full brightness. Scientists were unable to explain the phenomena, quieting people's questions with vague answers of client change as dusk fell earlier each day. Deema could explain it all.

She took one last glance at the sky and stepped through the portal and home. It filled her with joy to be allowed back after her past bad decisions.

The faeries had faired well in the battle against Kasdeya's minions, but not a day went by the air in The Glen didn't ring with the clash of swords in preparation for the next battle. With Abaddon freed from his chains, another battle was imminent, and the side for the Light needed more warriors.

Deema headed straight for the infirmary where Queen Linette struggled to bounce back after a slice to her shoulder with a poisoned blade. Shayna fought her own uphill battle to recovery from her injuries. She'd been drained of her blood after a vampire bite, the blood cleansed, then added back into her body. Not an easy or unpainful task. In the meantime, guarding New York City had fallen on Deema's shoulders, and she wanted to give the task back to Shayna immediately.

She paused in the doorway of the infirmary and held her breath as Queen Linette handed her staff to Shayna. "I place The Glen and those of the fae world into your hands, Shayna. I may not regain my full strength and must use what little I have to oversee the making of new chains to bind Abaddon."

"No, my queen." Shayna stepped back, letting the staff fall to the marble floor with a clatter. "I cannot."

"You must." The queen fell back onto a mound of pillows. "I leave our people in good hands. Use—" She caught sight of Deema. "Ah, there she is. Come, my dear." She held out a trembling hand. "You must work by Shayna's side as she once did mine. Keep her safe."

Deema grasped the queen's hand and bowed. "I will do all in my power not to disappoint." She choked back a sob. They would not survive without their queen. She cursed Radella, the vampire bound in the dungeon. The undead woman could stay there for eternity as far as Deema cared.

"Good." The queen closed her eyes. "I leave in two day's time whether I am well or not. Evil waits for no one. Go, I must rest."

Deema picked up the staff and handed it to Shayna. "You can do this."

She shook her head, her eyes swimming with tears. "It isn't my place. I was not born to rule."

"It is now. For a time, at least." She closed Shayna's fingers around the staff. "I will help you." She bowed. "My queen."

A sob escaped Shayna. "Do get up. We will reign together."

Deema glanced up. "Already the light around you glows brighter." She smiled. "Just don't let it go to your head."

Shayna gave a shuddery laugh. "I'm sure you will keep me in my place. Shall we let our friends know?" Her eyes widened. "Am I allowed to leave this place?"

Queen Linette chuckled. "You are queen. You may do as you please as long as matters are cared for here first. The Glen is your top priority." She waved a weak hand. "I know I handed over my staff, but I did ask you to leave so I may rest."

"We will go." Deema gave Shayna a nudge toward the door, eager to see Clark Payson, her favorite of the three human detectives who help the fae.

Faerie after faerie bowed as the two walked by. The staff clutched in Shayna's hand was all they needed in order to know the reign of power rested with another.

At the entrance to the portal, Shayna stopped and glanced at the staff. "I cannot take this with me, can I?"

Deema shrugged. "Maybe it turns to something else in the human world. Let's see."

With a nod, Shayna stepped into the portal and came out in Central Park New York City. She now clutched a blue umbrella and laughed. "Not a cloud in the sky, and I'll have to carry this. Doesn't go with the whole Special Agent façade, does it?"

"Humans are strange creatures. You'll get a look or two and nothing more." Deema grabbed her hand and teleported them to Shayna's hotel room where the witch, Agatha, engaged in her favorite pastime. Watching talk shows on television.

She glanced up. "You're back. It's good to see you." She flashed a snaggle-toothed grin. "What's on the agenda for today?" Her gaze fell on the umbrella in Shayna's hand and widened. She flicked off the television and bowed her head. "Queen."

"Please don't put on any pretenses for me. I'm not your queen."

"But you are a queen. Did Linette die?"

"No, she's occupied with other things. Let's

visit the precinct, shall we? I need to let Pierce know of this change."

"Most definitely." Agatha changed into a large rottweiler and stood still while Shayna clipped a leash around her neck. Purely pretense, as it usually trailed on the ground behind them, but humans jumped back in fear when they caught sight of the large, unleashed dog.

Deema's best friend might now rule the fae world, and she would be stretched between ridding the human world of darkness and ruling the world of the fae, but she was still Shayna, warrior of the Light. For this, Deema was grateful. There was no other warrior as powerful except for Alvar, the traitor.

Rather than teleport to the precinct and shock those who didn't know who they really were, Deema hailed a cab. The driver cast a wary glance at Agatha, but allowed them inside the vehicle. Agatha bared her teeth and leaped into the front passenger seat.

Deema laughed. She loved the feisty, ancient, witch who enjoyed terrifying others, but had a warrior's heart.

Shayna

Reigning queen. Shayna's insides quivered. She'd thought being the queen's top warrior was a challenge.

While Deema went to find Payson, and Agatha plopped down in the staff lounge to intimidate the uniformed officers, Shayna stopped in Pierce's doorway and watched him. He sat with his back to the door, phone to his ear. She loved this man with every fiber of her being. Just when she'd made the choice to bind herself to him after the final battle was fought, she became queen. Now was not the time for further entanglements, nor was it allowed.

"I told you to take care of the dispute earlier this morning! If a woman is hurt because of your incompetence, I'll feed your head to Agent Sky's dog." He slammed the receiver down and turned, his face breaking into a grin. Without hesitation he got to his feet, pulled her further into the room, and closed the door. "You're here."

"I am." She leaned into him as his arms folded around her. "I've missed you."

"I've been busy." He tilted her face to his. "Are you alright? I've stopped in The Glen every day at the infirmary, but most times you slept."

"I'm fine, but you may want to sit down." She gave a trembling smile.

"O-kay." He resumed his seat, folding his hands on his desktop while Shayna sat across from him.

She took a deep breath. "Queen Linette handed over her staff."

He sat back. "To whom?"

"Me."

He paled. "You're the fae queen?"

She nodded.

"How do I act? Do I bow?"

"If you do I'll strike you with my staff." She held up the umbrella. "Don't treat me any different. Just think of it as an added responsibility loaded onto my already heavy shoulders."

"A rather large responsibility." He laughed, his eyes twinkling. "I'm now the chief-of-police, and you're the queen. Watch out worlds." His smile faded. "I can't help but think this doesn't bode well for our relationship."

"It—"

"Chief." The receptionist, another new one, this time a woman around the age of fifty and very competent instead of an empty-headed Barbie doll he'd had in the past, interrupted via the phone intercom. "We've a riot outside. Shows promise of being nasty."

"And not human," Shayna said. She didn't need to look outside to know the trouble had started fresh upon her arrival.

"Thank you, Mary Ann." Pierce grabbed his jacket from the back of his chair.

Him and Shayna joined the others in a rush toward the front doors. "They can't come in," Shayna said. "The holy water Pierce doused the place with before the battle will keep them away, but there are plenty of people in danger outside." Pedestrians were drawn to anything out of the ordinary and sometimes got in the way of their own protection. She glanced at Mary Ann. "Bolt these doors. Do not open them for any reason. If we need medical attention, we have phones."

"Officer Charges, keep the uniforms inside to protect the civilians. Let no one other than us five in until I flash my badge," Pierce said. "Understood?"

"But, sir, we can help."

"Not this time."

Shayna heard the click of the door locking behind them. She'd have to do some damage control with those in and out of the building after they cleared the sidewalk, but it wasn't the first time. Things would be much simpler if she could show her true race. "The rest of you stay back unless I need you."

"Shayna…" Pierce narrowed his eyes.

She gave him a look that allowed no argument, then turned to face the crowd.

Alvar stood next to a man who stood well over six-feet-tall. Behind them stood several vampires. "Hello, Queen Shayna. Yes, word does travel fast." He glanced at the umbrella in her hand. "Meet my new friend, Linc. We needed someone else on our side to lead the lesser minions after you captured Radella. I wonder why you haven't killed her."

"What do you want?" Shayna crossed her arms and drew down to her side, donning her armor.

"While you are beautiful and fierce," he said, "your armor does not intimidate me, nor does Deema and the three humans wearing theirs. I've armor of my own should I choose to wear it." He glanced at Agatha. "I see you have a shifter of your own. Impressive size for a dog, but no match for my pet. Show them."

Linc changed to a black panther and showed his fangs.

"Again, I ask you what you want?" Shayna struck the tip of the umbrella against the sidewalk shooting sparks in every direction.

Alvar stepped back, his gaze widened.

"Afraid of a little bit of the Light?" Shayna grinned and struck harder, emitting a bright aura around herself. With the title of queen, came an increase to her powers.

All but Alvar stepped back several feet. "You cannot harm me with the Light."

"Oh, but I can." She moved forward. "When you turned traitor, you become weaker against the Light with each passing day. Soon you'll be no better than the foul demon you follow."

He continued backward as she slowly advanced. When a tree blocked him, he waved a hand at Linc. "Show her what you're capable of."

The shifter charged, faster than any animal in the natural kingdom. Shayna snapped her fingers when Agatha started to advance, stopping the witch, and stepped to the side to avoid the shifter.

Linc met dead air, sliding across the pavement. Crouching, he turned to spring again. "You're fast," he purred. "But, I'm faster."

"Really?" Shayna shot a blue lazer from her hand, freezing the shifter in place. "Your pet kitty is no match for my magic now that I am Queen." She smiled at Alvar. "Would you like to try again?"

"You'll regret ever accepting that staff." He put a hand on the panther's head and teleported them both away.

Shayna turned to the vampires. "Well? Are you staying to fight?"

They shrugged and darted away.

Shayna held up a hand at the civilians watching everything from a few feet away. "Filming a movie, folks. Nothing more than smoke and mirrors." She smiled and led her group back to the building to the sound of applause.

www.ingramcontent.com/pod-product-compliance
Lightning Source LLC
Chambersburg PA
CBHW061028120726

47910CB00006B/2141